MADE IN HERO

~

THE WAR FOR SOAP

Library of Congress Control Number: 2007903876

Hugh, Betty.

Made in Hero: the War for Soap / Betty Hugh.

ISBN-10:   0-9796603-8-6

ISBN-13:   978-0-9796603-8-2

Classical/Allegorical/Literary—Fiction.

Printed in the United States of America.

Illustrations and book design by Betty Hugh

Clay Dog Books
P.O. Box 600295
Newton, MA 02460

www.claydogbooks.com

for soap soldiers

Made in Hero

The War for Soap

BETTY HUGH

clay dog
books

Contents

PROLOGUE

PRIMAL SCREAM

HILL SIDE, Hero — I sit in my rented room with the lights out; nothing running but the fans. They make the noise of electric bellows, heaving in a mechanical rhythm to no particular beat. Three of them are pointed at my head from different angles, their irate forces tangling in a whirlwind. But they offer no relief. The heat, packing its sour sweet odor, throbs to its own pulse, and drives me to wonder if it was all an accident that my writing of the war had turned into the story of a corpse.

Maybe it was just one more bizarre twist in the labyrinth, a little like taking a wrong turn. On the other hand, when it comes to "right turns" in the labyrinth, there may be no such thing. Okay, if my puns are getting weak at this stage, it's because I'm manic. I'm out of my skin. And in the end, the reason for writing is not what I thought it was. It is not the knight's quest for truth. It is the cave man's primal scream into the darkness.

Our scream belched straight out of the cosmic dust storm. It swept up unbolted pieces of the universe which, like bolls of pollen, had nothing to do but bounce along. In the whirlwind, it took on the properties of a magnet, sucking up flecks of shell and metallic debris. Heated to combustion, the scream found expression in its own catastrophe.

Since then, humanity has been unable to resist the strain. Undaunted, it proceeded to carve its own niche in the wasteland. Established by a society of nomads, the early colony was an unassuming patch of sand beginning at the coincidence of sunrise with the mouth of a river. At the opposite end, the sands converged to a quarry which, by its very aspect, inspired forethoughts of a repository for ghosts. More than that, Hero, at the beginning, was a transient and mute idea. Inspiring a species who divines its own death, then lives to tell it, it evolved to a people judged less by the lives they live than by how they are treating the dead.

Today, Hero proclaims itself a nation within a city, a modern Troy under siege. Technology—that wooden horse so long ago foretold—infiltrates it at the seams, producing highways dotted with strip malls where once there had been boulevards of cobblestone lined with awnings and the wispy light vapors of trees. Modernity floods the marketplace with useless gadgets everyone professes not to want, yet line up at Saturday shops to purchase on credit.

By now, the originating waterway has left no evidence, having dissolved from the invisible source from which it flowed. And yet, even as the sands were drying, the city itself took root, nourished with fresh ideas of its own identity. As trees have been seen to spring from the surface of boulders, it continues to thrive on land increasingly isolated by its own thirst; isolated, too, by its clamp-like grip on a distant, ever-receding past. The Hero of today pulls itself from the rock and struts about, a mighty sphinx swaying in the heat of its own belabored footsteps, its stone claws ill-equipped to swat away the flies, or even the ghosts of those who dared to dream it into being.

PART 1

STONES

CHAPTER ONE

FURIES

SAND STORM

OLD CITY, Hero — On the morning his assassins were preparing to kill him, the Commander awoke earlier than he otherwise might have. He was aware of doing it for no reason other than to observe the first blushing streaks of the sun. Thus, when the breezes began blowing in from the desert, he went to the open window in order to inhale deeply the soft gusts riding the tail of the sand storm. Three days had lain smothered under its curtain before any visible lifting of the dust. Then, just after sunset of the prior evening, the sands summarily vanished, leaving no more trace of themselves than they had given warning of their coming. A meteorologist I spoke to hailed the event as "the most severe in collective memory"—as in, the virtual public vault where all records of the kind are kept. That's a way of saying, as disclaimers go, that Heroaen science renounces the time-proven practice of paper-and-ink.

At the window, air wet the Commander's palette with a desolate fragrance that brought up the vague remembrance of lilies. This purified him; even made him a little bit dizzy. He pulled on a pale shirt of linen, drew it down over his head and the bulk of his shoulders, then absently tucked the excess folds into the waist of his pants. Crisp as new laundry, the cloth crackled with the closure of the buttons. He'd given no explanation for the sudden visit to his mother, at a home he'd long taken the precaution of avoiding. When I asked her about it later, she said she'd simply attributed his appearance to the timing of the sand storm—serendipitous as events around here go. She remembered only that, before stepping away from the second story window, he took a final, measured glance down the narrowness of the path below.

HERO

I have come to believe that from the time he was a boy, the Commander must have known how brutally his enemies would hunt in order to kill him. He would know it as surely as he knew the placement of each stone in the cobble pattern of the street. Since the beginning, his path had been laid out by the stones, their rough surfaces marking the trail, leading him closer to that momentous destination. What would take him by surprise was the indirectness of the route. It would wind past the doorsteps of countless neighbors, many of whose houses he has slept in. At each door, he would raise a tremulous uproar with the pounding of his fists. But with the assassins closing in, he would not be able to wait the time any of the neighbors were taking to answer. Instead, he would run, and keep on running, each step taking him deeper into the labyrinthine alleys. Above them, just inside the balcony of one of the buildings, a girl was sleeping, blissfully unaware of the incident unfolding in the streets below. He had no way of knowing, perhaps, how she would determine his redemption—with an idea so defiant, and altogether peculiar, that she alone could have conceived it. He understood even less that it was she, and not his enemies, who held the power to transform him into a martyr (an outcome they were powerless to suppress). All his life, however, he, as well as plenty of those who knew him, were convinced that he was headed for nothing but trouble. His mother recalled, "Nothing interested him so much as taking up the stones." But neither his mother, or the girl, or for that matter, any other of those who knew him, had foreseen the tumultuous events that would haunt the immediate aftermath of his death. The ensuing riots had no less effect than to convulse the streets of Hero. They had the additional impact of luring me back.

STRINGS

Three years ago, my first stay in Hero was brief—just a drop-in to cover for a wounded colleague. Pea Nuts, as we called him (and this was a term of endearment he'd deliberately adopted), was Editor-in-Chief of the Heroaen bureau. Seven years prior, he'd established that modest office and became its sole staff member. In spite of the bureau's humble beginnings, however, Pea Nuts had always treated Hero as his baby—or his monster. In the intervening years, he'd nurtured it like a delicate plant (a natural task for someone adept at growing cannabis under fluorescent lightbulbs). As fate would have it, the monster responded beautifully to his tender care, maturing into one of The Chronicle's headiest spots for international news (it's true; all the world loves a conflict). Three years ago when I saw him, Pea Nuts was lying in the hospital, all patched up. I said, "Pea Nuts, you look like a scarecrow—and not an especially neat one." He said, "Welcome to Hero." Pea Nuts had been partially blown up by a bomb. Presumably, it was planted in the Hall of Governors by Heroaen militants—with several groups competing for the credit. So, during the weeks that Pea Nuts worked at growing his skin back, I covered his stories.

I was glad to do it, considering all that I owed him, say, for certain embarrassing instances. Once, during a botched coup in the tropics, I got caught at a roadblock with a truckload of rebels (that's what I got for accepting the ride—and they were card sharks, every last man). The loyalist troops who arrested us were so annoyed they confiscated my papers and tossed me into the hole (my press cards did not impress them). Pea Nuts helicoptered in from the next country over. It took him twenty-nine phone calls and an emergency visit to the Consulate General to finally bail me out. There were other occasions—too numerous to list. More importantly though, there was the tug of invisible strings that recognized no geographical walls. Pea Nuts called us the "train tracks"— two crooked paths of a set of parallel rails.

We had started together as novice reporters. To us, The Chronicle—an expanding global newspaper—had all the appeal of a wayward adventure. Eager to cut our teeth in some of the world's least congenial places, we went wherever The Chronicle decided to send us. For years thereafter, I'd run into Pea Nuts in the flee hotels of yet another developing country. He would always look the same, though with more or less facial hair depending on the climate (until he adopted a permanent goatee). Like radar, we'd locate the nearest saloon, toast our past and recent exploits, and form the joint opinion that all the separate wars we saw were adding up to one large, indistinguishable war. Like orphaned twins, we've been writing that war ever since.

That's not to say that change doesn't happen. Namely, we got older. More to the point, Pea Nuts' rail would split off in a different direction from mine. I even remember the exact moment of the split. It happened when I encountered him on an island hideout growing maudlin over a glass of the foulest scotch. "One year at a time, Teheda, that's how we do this. But have you noticed, the world never stops?" He considered me at length, then blurted, "That doesn't bother you, does it?" Apparently, my wherever-life-takes-me attitude had earned me the reputation of a fatalist. No doubt, Pea Nuts was determined to take charge of his own course. He announced his intention of settling down somewhere, of finding a home. But then, it takes a guy like Pea Nuts to make his home in a place like Hero. A few months later, that's precisely where he went. I got the postcard.

Pea Nuts had coordinated his arrival with what is now known throughout the region—and not without affection—as The Great Uprising. Over seven years in duration, GU would surge over the borders of at least three nations, and rip through the economies of countless others. It had magnificent range. In short, GU would destabilize The Empire nearly to the point of collapse (some of its instigators anointed themselves the "New Barbarians"). More remarkable, however, was that GU had fomented in the seemingly insignificant streets of Hero—a locale The Empire had largely considered a remote, forsaken outpost. Pea Nuts, on the other hand, at once glimpsed Hero's hidden potential. He even went as far as to forecast that this small, struggling nation would become one of the next decade's hottest spots of conflict. Like a mad scientist, he declared his determination to "put Hero on the news map." So leasing a dilapidated warehouse, Pea Nuts hailed The Chronicle as the first foreign news agency to establish a Heroaen bureau, with Pea Nuts himself at the helm. Since that time, The Chronicle has seen the rise of a host of copycat rivals—ample proof that Pea Nuts' gamble on the bureau paid off. According to promise, he'd put Hero on the news map.

When the militants bombed him, Pea Nuts again sent me a postcard. Would I come to cover the bureau, he asked, with the added appeal that Hero was just starting to get interesting. It was the year of the internationally brokered peace talks. Many hoped that, in spite of the occasional spikes in violence, the fractious rebel groups were in fact preparing to lay down their weapons. Among all parties, there seemed a genuine longing to bring final closure to GU. For press types everywhere, this represented a milestone—even to a jaded reporter like me. So at Pea Nuts' request, I came to Hero and stayed a mind-spinning ninety-three days. Working round the clock, I vaulted from government office to government office, from there to the embassies, to the hospitals, to security checkpoints, and back to the government offices. In addition to performing such chief's duties as signing paychecks and deciding what was newsworthy, I filed story after story. Mostly, these consisted of news bites—cranked-out pieces rich in drama, poor in depth. The whole time, I experienced no more of local life than I could glimpse out the window of a speeding taxi.

But before departing, I would conduct an unprecedented— and clandestine—interview with one of Hero's most elusive militia commanders. The resulting full-length feature would win acclaim as the bureau's widest read story of the year. Over time, of course, the piece was destined to be absorbed back into the fog of so much GU coverage. And it would be dwarfed by larger fires flickering elsewhere in the world, raging in larger theaters, and for higher global stakes. I'd be there to cover those, too. And yet, geography and distance notwithstanding, Hero never quite left me. Subjected to the briefest exposure, I was already sharing the symptoms of Pea Nuts' strange fever. Like a virus, or a cause, Hero is infectious.

As I wander, today, the narrow streets, I am astonished by the sense that time, throughout the ages, has made no movement here. Hero really is Eden. My eyes scour the same sights they may have recorded from the beginning—the heavy wooden doors painted powder colors, wagons still drawn by donkeys, and the oddness of burning rubber tires thrown into the middle of the road. My nose registers the pungent aroma of meats roasting at the carts of the street peddlers. And at a certain hour of the afternoon, I am seduced, my resistance broken, by the scent of coffee—made here like no place else in the world. As I turn the corner, I suddenly find myself pelted by the familiar onslaught of rocks and pebbles. Children throw them against senseless, impenetrable targets, and at each other. Rock throwing, like coffee, long ago evolved into an art form in this ancient town. Every day I am caught in the cross fire. I choke on the same dust.

FROM THE OUTSET, I understood that I'd come back to investigate the death of the Commander, the circumstances precipitating it, as well as the events which immediately followed—increasingly referred to as GU-2 (rebellions here have a way of recycling themselves). But I realized, and only after a period of catastrophic reflection, that my real purpose was to tell the story of his life. I did not foresee how much this purpose was to become my obsession, until something odd happened one evening while stepping over the city's crumbling cobbled pavements. Crunching underfoot, they recalled to me that Heroaens have a saying, "If the stones could speak, what story would they be telling?" It occurred to me that the Commander's life was none other than the story of the stones.

Over time, too, I'd come to realize that my responsibility was greater than it initially appeared. It involved no mere examination of the current revolt, but rather the attempt to explain it in terms of the larger war the reading public is all but sick of. And there lies my dejection. Even for myself, the war grows tiresome. I have been writing it too long. The recent violence strikes me simply as an echo of that larger, interminable conflict.

Forlorn, I summed up the work that lay ahead—a relentless pursuit of illusory facts, the untangling of rumor, the endless rummaging through details so trivial they slip through the tension of the fingers. Clawing, I entered the labyrinth. In the beginning, this meant going to the street. There I was told, by anonymous voices, that the man killed was a martyr, a champion of the cause, defender of the people. From others, I heard he was a victim of the system. Somewhere in this chaos began the emergence of clarity. There had been not one crime, but many. Layers and layers of them. Yet my job remained the sorting of the one: the burial of the body of an outlaw. I understand now that this crime, in its simplicity, was the true beginning, not the ending, to the story. And yet, it was a beginning that hurled me nowhere but into the past. That is the place where time becomes inverted, and must be turned, like a bloodstained garment, inside out. Grasping at the sleeves, I would eventually come to my most significant realization.

I had known the man.

It was a recognition, however, that unlike the body, was to remain buried for a good length of time. The fact remained that, as it lay stretched upon a slab in the municipal morgue, I myself had the opportunity to view the slain man's corpse without the faintest recollection of ever having met him. Our prior acquaintance had been fleeting and, at best, partial. In all, I never got a look at his face.

LEMONS

"Your job is easy," I was told—with all the frankness of a man who should know. He went by the name of Dusty, and was Chief Editor of Chronicle's International Desk when Pea Nuts and I first came on. "Just write what you see," he said, "and not what you went in expecting." Then, somewhat evilly, he would tag on the warning, "So long as you keep in mind that, on the page, there is no place to hide." In its stark, unforgiving way, Dusty's was the first advice I found useful. More than advice, it was his personal mantra of integrity, and to this day, I think of it every time I embark on a new assignment—however mundane or apocalyptic. In Hero, it can be difficult to tell the difference.

By the third hour of afternoon, an eerie quiet had set in on the street. Surveying the carnage of soot and garbage, I was reminded of yet another of Dusty's warnings. "Your sole purpose is to record the truth," he said, and by that, he meant "a piece of it." In practical terms, this requires raking up some detail which could appear significant on the page. It may be the off-hand remark expressed by a weary combatant, a dazed victim, or a scavenging, elderly woman. It may be the high pitched bark of a dog. Possibly, it is the fatness of the flies swarming in the hollow of an eye socket, bleached colorless by the sun. And if it isn't a quote or image, it may be nothing more than the mark of punctuation at the end of a three-word sentence. But it is just that. A detail. "Don't think of injecting the story with a meaning, either," Dusty added, "because you can just forget it. That stuff, you keep to yourself. Out there, you're just a grunt, Teheda." He'd wait until I got one foot out the door, then grumble to my back, "Remember, just get the dispatch."

I'd be left wondering if he meant grunt, as in, "not entitled to an opinion;" or grunt, as in, "follow your orders and don't ask questions." The latter puzzled me only because I was operating under the assumption that asking questions was the whole point of my job. Years later and now a veteran reporter, I still haven't totally worked it out. In any case, in the middle of a ravaged street in Hero, this grunt had set out to collect another small piece of the truth.

At the start, I discovered that the face of war is a child. This doesn't say much (as observations go), because the impression is wholly predictable. It is always like this. The children gather in clusters, huddling in doorways, or beneath the crooked shadows of light posts. Their faces are usually blank. If they express anything at all, it is curiosity more than terror—which leads to the second little truth: innocence is first lost among the young.

I advanced a few more paces. As the soles of my shoes bristled over gravel that was formerly pavement (at least at one time), I scratched into my notebook a permanent record of the bizarre yet familiar sights and sounds. Haze, smoke, and the shriveling odor of cement and ashes took their rightful positions at the top of the list. Beneath them I added the wafting of rotting citrus and then, the perfume drift of lilacs—though that's impossible here. By law, Hero is a flower-free zone. Of course, it's also the kind of place where a confusion of the senses is perfectly normal.

Cautiously, I rounded the corner, eyes scanning the array of broken windows above the sidewalk. I recorded them. Looking up again, I searched tirelessly for movement in the places where it is most unlikely (and where you usually find it). But sometimes, you just don't.

And then, I saw the girl. Fuzzy, raw and sooty, her presence could at any moment turn to vapor, or vanish from recognition because I'd come across her too many times, in too many varied locations, and that's no lie. I have seen this girl—in some shape or form—in every location I've ever stepped foot, as if she were a piece of me, or had attached herself to the contents of my luggage. The problem with Familiar is how easily it passes for Invisible. Had the girl not been the only person on the street, I ran the risk of stepping over her—without so much as seeing. But on this day, haphazardly, I opened my eyes. She was hawking lemons salvaged from the rubble of the riots. Raising one toward me with an open fist, she began to shake it. I decided, for the moment, to ignore the gesture. Instead, I assailed her with the usual questions.

"What did you see?"

Without answering, she kept shaking the lemon.

"Can you tell me where you were when the rioting happened?"

When she wouldn't, I plied her with a few more questions.

Finally, I asked "Which side started the fighting?" (always a good one).

Now it was her head that was shaking, and not the lemon. That's how long it took me to figure out that the girl was mute—speaking not with voice, but with the lemon. She went back to shaking it. Her eyes were wide—swelled up with insistence, persuasion, and hope. I pressed a crumpled paper into the outstretched palm of her hand—Heroaen currency. Transfixed, I watched her fingers make a fist around the dollar, then left without taking her lemon. Walking, I turned toward the skyline looming in the distance. My ears strained to hear the ripple of human voices I'd been half expecting. But the only sound was the crisp barking of a dog.

Dusty was right. The story is seldom what you think it will be. For sure, there's no point in trying to inject it with a meaning. What's more, I had failed to collect the eyewitness' statement I'd gone out to look for. And at the end of the day, I acknowledged once again that I'm really nothing more than a grunt.

What matters, though, is that I got the dispatch.

PEA NUTS' HUNCH

"TEHEDA, this is a load of crap."

As always, Pea Nuts tended toward an elegant choice of words.

"Writer's block?"

"Well, uh..."

"I brought you back to cure you of that. Problem is, you're still looking for secrets, decoding meanings that never were there. It's just news, Pal."

I scratched the back of my ear, mumbling, "You may have a point there."

"Of course I have a point. It's your story that didn't. Try bringing back something I can use...upturned cars, a shootout—before we start losing the readership, and after that, the advertisers. Look, will you do me a favor?"

"I know, Pea Nuts."

"Just get the dispatch. And remember, it's only the news."

WE DECIDED TO MOVE our conversation to Zax—the watering hole conveniently located across the street. Its principle business is catering to the delinquencies of foreign journalists. Like in a movie set, we passed through the swinging shutter-style doors (sort of "retro-saloon"). I half expected a woman to show up in a hot pink bordello outfit, but was disappointed. She didn't arrive. Meanwhile, we swaggered straight to the back of the room to claim the corner booth where, three years ago, Pea Nuts had urged me, by way of a farewell toast, "Try not to miss hell too much." (Still convalescing from burns, he was taking his liquid through a straw inserted into a temporary helmet made of gauze. It didn't curb his thirst any.) In celebration of our reunion, Pea Nuts ordered me a bourbon and himself a scotch to go along with the table snack that was his namesake. Comfortably settled, he wasted no time starting in.

"Teheda, what worries me is your penchant for writing about nothing. It's getting worse. What's that about, anyway?"

"I don't know."

"I heard you tried to leave the business. That surprised me at first. Then I got to thinking, it was like the time I got off the plane and decided to stay here—anywhere—for good."

If you didn't know Pea Nuts, the decision might have been puzzling. At the time, Hero had all the attraction of a frumpy backwoods district, gripped in a war not many people in the world cared about. He had justified it in terms of his ambition to strike out on his own, launch his own bureau, establish a permanent address. But I suspected murkier, heart-of-darkness kinds of reasons. And I still do.

"Putting down roots was my way of dropping out too," he maintained. "Teheda, I guess it was just your turn."

"I wanted to spend more time on the other side of the planet," I agreed, "—where they don't give a rat's ass about this or any other war, where they don't even care enough to read the paper. I wanted to forget everything I'd seen or written— and be a happy man."

"Well, what happened?"

"I don't know. A lot of things. Mostly, I couldn't cope with the happy."

Mostly, I blamed the unbearable normalcy of my life. Back home, I got bored reporting celebrity gossip—which lost its fun after a while—or investigating the tax-evading practices of the rich. Peace-time journalism had struck me as, well, mundane.

"I didn't think you'd last a day out there. Admit it. We need this rat's ass." He threw down his scotch and called for another. Then he doubled back to his mission statement of saving me from my own demons. "Really though—I'm concerned for you. Coming back is just the beginning. You're still walking around like some kind of novel without a plot."

"That's good, Pea Nuts."

"I'm serious, Pal."

I also hate it when he calls me "Pal." It's always a sign that more of his concern is coming...

"Your work is beginning to sound like one long run-on sentence..."

Yeah, like Pea Nuts, who just keeps going, and going...

"'Beggar Girl with Lemon,'" he sneered. "I send you to a riot, and that's what you come back with. It's cute, but is it journalism? Listen now. I have a job, and you have a job. And we both know nonsense won't make the headlines."

"Okay, I get it."

"But do you?"

"I'll work on it."

"For a fact, you will—because I'm sending you on another assignment. And don't think it isn't a favor."

"I won't forget that, Pea Nuts."

"Well then, do me a favor. Try to bring back a story this time—something big, something hot. I want it on fire."

WHERE HE SENT ME was the municipal morgue.

Pea Nuts' greatest talent is timing. Like a hound trained to sniff out explosives, he senses incendiary events days before they are scheduled to happen. Thus, even as we sat over our glasses at Zax, Pea Nuts had been mulling over the likelihood that the municipal morgue would become the next breaking story. "You really want me to go to the morgue?" I'd balked. "That's a hell of a place to pick up a story, Pea Nuts."

"It's the favorite spot for crowds these days."

"Crowds in Hero? That's not news."

"Well, at the morgue, they are starting to get edgy."

"They've been there for the past six days. So what if the occasional stone goes flying? This is Hero."

"I figured you'd say that. Why do you think I brought you back?"

I stewed over that for a minute, then sighed and slammed down the rest of my beverage.

"Look, if it's stones you want, it's stones you'll get."

"Stones are fine, Teheda. Just don't bring them back without a story."

CHAPTER TWO

INSIDERS

LATE AFTERNOONS

EAST SQUARE, Hero — Late afternoons here are basked in an iridescent blue-gray light sprinkled with patches of orange. It is dreamlike, hedging on idyllic, if not for the cool, distant flatness of the source. The retiring sun, conspicuously hidden, casts long shadows upon a city plaza mysteriously empty of people. Perhaps it—the light, or the emptiness—was also the source of my foreboding—the incidental spooky feeling that I'd already experienced this moment and had merely dropped by for yet another revisit.

Crossing The Square, I bypassed the looming obelisk that was its centerpiece before arriving at the southeast corner, really more a synaptic junction formed by the clearing between two streets. Buildings dotting their length were modest in scale, almost accidental, as if ambivalent of their positions within the space—and uncertain whether to be quaint or ominous. They seemed in danger of being misplaced—maybe lost, forever— the next time I carelessly sneezed or blinked. But if dislocation was the scenic effect, it would be confounded by the next element to come into my view. In the distance, a tree appeared to spring up from an otherwise vacant lot. Solitary and central, it offered neither apology, nor explanation. What it suggested, to the contrary, was a rooting to the reality of things. Its only flaw, or where it fell short of entirely convincing, was that some of its branches were eclipsed by the frame of the door.

Yes, I really did say "door." More accurately, it is a solid wall with an arch punched through it. I've seen many relics of this kind in Hero, yet no one I've asked seems to know their purpose. Warily, I wager my own guess that their reason for existence is symbolic, rather than practical. This example, planted smack in the middle of the junction, marks a sojourner's passage from one side of street to the other, neither entering nor departing a building in between. Impolitely speaking, it is something like a fake doorway. But call it a symbol or call it an illusion, one thing that is certain is that, structurally speaking, The Door has stood its ground. What it accomplished, additionally, was to deflect my attention from the tree—whose presence I still hadn't determined for real. Fact or phantom, I now remembered it as the original (true) subject of my gaze.

Well, if my afternoon—and the tree—had so far been delusional, their unreality would culminate in the form of the next solid mass. Not surprisingly, it loomed in the compressible space between myself and the tree. A stout building, it struck me as an enormous face with a clock affixed to its forehead, above and between where the eyes would be. Without a doubt, this had to be the morgue.

The clock, with its calibrated dial and bony fingers, pointed away the minutes in conjunction with the rapid departure of the light. Dusk was quickly asserting its claim. More hurriedly, then, I emerged from the arch of the dividing wall—The Door—and effectively passed into the other side of the street. Within a few paces, I confronted the front portal of the morgue. And, with a sweeping glance to the side, my eyes confirmed the de facto position of the tree—just moments ago, a phantom. As it turned out, the two elements stood opposite each other—

in direct relation. Whether their respective placements had been random or deliberate, the effect was the same. A little bit startling. Moreover, the onset of dusk aggravated the elongation of their shadows.

Heightening matters, I soon discovered that we were not alone, neither the building, the tree, myself—or our shadows. From the corner of my eye, I saw that we'd been joined by additional shadows, supplemented by a faint drift of voices. Tracking them like audible foot prints, I came around to the back side of the building, where my path was immediately cut off by a gate. Partially eaten by rust, its vertical bars yet stood dignified and erect, like members of a doomed honor guard. A few yards beyond the soldered hinges, the split of the gate was reinforced—strangled, really—by a heavy chain necklace strung with a series of padlocks.

I arrived just in time to observe the morgue watchman turn his back on the leftover demonstrators. He mounted the steps to the dock (a platform jutting from the rear door), and receded safely to the interior of the building. "We've been here seven days," a man on the street informed me. "This is how it always ends." And then, as if to exacerbate my letdown, he added, "But if you'd have come an hour ago…"

Sure. Unlike Pea Nuts', my own clock seems timed in order to miss things. In this case, it was the carting away by police of a handful of overzealous protesters. "Military vans, sirens, handcuffs," the man listed, and finally, the familiar word, "stones."

"Did you see the number wounded?" I pried; then, with about as much delicacy as a jackal, "Any dead?"

"Dead?" the man repeated wryly. "If it's the dead you're after, did you know we're in front of the morgue?"

Heroaen sarcasm aside, it struck me as a very good question. Until that afternoon, in fact, I had given the morgue little consideration, in spite of my awareness that the body of the slain commander lay inside. Typically, the remains of deceased Heroaens are held over in the municipal morgue for twenty-four hours in order to be processed (in Hero, even death involves paperwork; and rebels are not exempt). Only after such administrative detail is the body released to members of the deceased person's family, who, by that time, are anxious to get on with the traditional rites of burial. The problem with the case of the rebel commander was that a full week had passed—well exceeding the standard twenty-four hours.

Meanwhile, outside the morgue the protests persisted with each passing day. Inconspicuously, they had started with a small contingent of the slain man's relatives, associates, and neighbors who, after waiting at the dock in excess of eight hours, were addressed by a spokesman. On this day, like all the previous days, he dismissed them. "We didn't come here to make trouble," a woman in the group told me. "We only came to collect the body."

BACK AT THE PRESS OFFICE, I found Pea Nuts curled over his keyboard in the standard editor's posture, eyeballs hungrily scanning lines of text across the screen.

"Still here?" I noted, without the slightest trace of surprise. "Pea Nuts, it's 9 PM. Don't you have somewhere to go?"

Of course, for Pea Nuts, it's never too late for a briefing.

"What was the deal at the dead joint?"

"No deal. Stalemate. Disgruntled citizens milling around. I missed a few stones getting projectiled."

"That's funny," he said. "I really had an instinct."

More funny to me was how much his "instinct" had passed for expectation; namely, that I'd accomplish no less than to steal fire and bring it back from the clouds. Of course, the only thing on fire at the scene had been the occasional rubber tires that had been stripped from cars, lit, and tossed randomly into the middle of the road. Their placement appeared random, anyway. More likely, they'd been purposefully thrown out by the crowds to slow down the intervention of police—as a sort of poor man's roadblock. As such solutions go, the tires were largely ineffective. By the time I arrived, Security Forces had already dispersed the demonstrators and cordoned off the area with streams of shiny yellow tape. I said, "It looks like your famous timing misfired on this one. It happens. But Pea Nuts, I tried to tell you…"

"Never mind, Teheda. I've gotta another one for you…"

He sent me straight from the morgue into even deeper bowels of the Heroaen Purgatory—a virtual holding cell for saints and sinners, alike. In the morning, I'd be going to the notorious Hero prison—where a disproportionate number of Heroaen men are obliged, at some point in their lives, to be incarcerated.

HUNGER STRIKE

A central condition of prison life was disclosed to me within minutes of my opening conversation with one of the inmates.

"For my first dinner here, the guard handed me half a loaf of flatbread, a fistful of raw almonds, and three olives," he said, "when what I really need is a woman's cooking."

"Can't you protest?" I asked.

"You mean organize a hunger strike?" he quipped, waving away my suggestion with hands that were bound together at the wrists. "You don't understand," he explained. "It has gotten better this time around. *They have added the olives.*"

Considering that he was, in fact, the ringleader behind the current hunger strike, his sense of irony was keen. I quickly surmised that refusing food must be what he had in mind from the very beginning. He had been in detention barely a week. Yet within that time span, he'd already led the fifty men of his own and neighboring cells into a standard revolt—the kind that is easily and instantly crushed by an overstaffed prison security force. He must have known that violent rebellion did not stand a chance. Rather, it had given way to a collective hunger strike eventually involving two hundred prisoners. Their demand, for all this trouble, was a simple daily ration of coffee.

"Why coffee?" I asked. "Why not something more substantial, like better food?"

He scoffed at the ridiculous nature of my question.

"Because coffee is more critical than food," he stated.

He was, of course, a native of Hero. Moreover, he was a man who'd been willfully refusing nourishment for days.

The prison did not issue uniforms, but instead allowed the inmates to retain the clothes they had come in with. Thus, the threadbare cloth of a shirt, blue though faded from perspiration, drooped against the prisoner's arms and shoulders. He was still a young man, and beneath the garment, I discerned bones incongruously large for the wasting flesh around them, on a body that, given more abundant circumstances, hinted at the musculature of an athlete.

I leaned into the bars to light his cigarette. I had obtained access to the prisoner only after protracted negotiations with the administrative office, resolved predictably by the passing of a courtesy fee into the hands of the warden. It was an unethical transaction that benefitted me greatly. I learned quickly that in the shady world of Hero prison, it is impossible to conduct an investigation of anything without the enthusiastic cooperation of the staff. In short, I've seen too many such institutions, and my experience as a correspondent long ago taught me that the shortest path between two points is a bribe. Unfailingly, the warden supplied not only the background of the current revolt, but the identity (and case history) of the man behind it.

Like so many of the men of Hero, he was already serving the second sentence of his life (or something like a second life sentence). The warriors of Hero begin their careers early. Incarcerated as a youth over a labor dispute, my prisoner had emerged from his first sentence with a debonair sense of savvy, a heightened political awareness, a sharpened instinct for survival, and most importantly—a nom de guerre. He explained that, as a youth inside the small cell he shared with twenty other men and boys, he'd come to the decision to adopt the name of Hektor. How he came upon the inspiration, he did not say. I asked the usual questions pertaining to political alliances, enmities, and personal entanglements—fishing for the lurid details that could make a feature article exciting. (Naturally, I was mindful of Pea Nuts' mandate, now seared into my conscience like a cow brand.) But Hektor was taciturn and cautious, revealing little. Men inside the prisons are often wary of how their words may be manipulated by the press. In all, we talked but a brief quarter of an hour before the guard on duty terminated our exchange, citing the demands of a heavily regimented prison schedule.

"I think that means his shift is over," Hektor said, "and he wants to go home."

"Even a prison guard has got a family," I pointed out.

"In his case, I hope it is a hundred bratty children."

"And a fat wife?" I suggested.

This image produced in him a gentle chuckle—in a display of spontaneity that seemed not to belong behind the cage-like bars. I was reminded that even a prisoner has got a sense of humor.

In the days ahead, I would learn that he was with the Commander on the night of his death. As early as our first interview, however, my instincts were already telling me that, in addition to the dead commander, the man who called himself Hektor was central to any story worth writing about the current upheaval.

"So, you want to know about me," he noted, "which means you'll be asking me to talk."

I recognized in his voice the boredom of a man who has endured too many questions.

"That means you want to get at my secrets," he continued. "For a fact, I've got more than a few."

I nodded, saying nothing while I watched him thinking. A bright flame lit the end of his cigarette as he took a prolonged drag, then held the fire for a moment on his tongue. Exhaling the plume of smoke, he resembled a dragon.

"Then promise me one thing. When our talking is over, just do a good job writing my life."

"I solemnly vow to try," I assured him.

And I meant it. Profoundly, I believed that the struggles of the man called Hektor were inseparable from those of the Commander whose fate would become my obsession; two lives defined by the kind of war I'd devoted so much of my own life attempting to write. Peering through the prison bars, I asked directly, "Do you consider yourself a hero?"

After thinking it over, he replied in a mild scowl, "What do you think?"

"You strike me as a man of quiet courage," I ventured, "and generally grumpy outlook."

This, too, provoked a sputter of laughter.

ENIGMA OF HERO

I once heard a riddle that all stories trace back to the source. In Hero, this can only mean going to the stones—the fragments of memory embedded in its history. Like pebbles, they have inflicted blisters at the bottoms of your feet. More specifically, any attempt to piece together the life of the Commander ought not to be attempted without a brief explanation of his birthplace; that is, of how the people of Hero came to be, in their unique sense, heroic.

The problem is that stones do not speak; not outright, anyway. And I am in a land where the past is passed from mouth to mouth—without a textbook. The library is of no use to me. Instead, I idle away hours sipping coffee at outdoor tables, clacking dice, loitering on street corners—any place where I can meet and talk to people. More importantly, I listen, trying my best to sort the bits of information I am given. But Hero is as much an idea as a location. The old dice players will tell you of a time that it did not appear on maps. Then, on a windless day ten years ago, it lost its anonymity forever.

Early in the morning, a group of striking farmers set torches to a government warehouse. Within the hour, cleanup crews had to scrape its contents from the ground. A thousand pounds of aromatic coffee—marked for export—had been reduced to an acrid tar. By afternoon, sporadic episodes of violence were engulfing even the quietest of streets. Combined, the events of that day would burgeon into an era—destined to be glorified as Hero's "Great Uprising." But this term invites examination. It results, in part, from the magical interplay of memory and language. When asked to describe the outbreak, residents often testify that it began much like any other day. (I am guessing here that, without the poetic phrase to immortalize it, the day might well have fizzled and passed into oblivion.) It is no secret, then, that words have power. Thus, with the first utterance of the term "Great Uprising," its onslaught was branded into memory. Vividly, Heroaens are now able to recall that opening day moment by moment, citing with astonishing precision where they were, with whom, and at what hour. Most can even tell how they became aware, gradually or all of a sudden, of the magnitude of events unfolding around them. From that collective memory (some claim hallucination), sprang a revolution of image—more than language, and not less than a poetry of the mind. From anonymous sources, its fever sparked and soon caught fire, sending up smoke that billowed over the mountains and covered the land, raining down like ashes. But if you really break it down, and in simple enough terms, you could say it all began with the inviolable image of a stone.

BOY WITH A STONE

It was cupped in the palm of his hand, cradled beneath the chubby fingers, its surface encrusted with traces of dirt. The boy reared back, gathering momentum from his heels up through the spine and shoulders. Uncoiling, he sprang forward, free-falling, unleashing pure velocity without the breaks. With a snap, the weighted object jolted into air, transforming itself to thunder. In flight, it painted a stroke across the sky. On the ground, the boy waited to hear its thud, assuring him of the certainty of its landing...somewhere over there. By the side of the road, I stood and waited, just as he did. In the unseen distance, the falling object pounded into earth, answering us with a dull, definitive echo. When the event was over, we heard again the silence; and wondered, as we do each time, where such might can come from that sleeps inside a simple stone.

The boy was not conscious of me, and was not the least concerned with the incident of my passing. On this morning, he'd been singularly absorbed in his effort, without distraction, of hurling the stone. Perhaps he had simply grown used to my momentary presence at that early hour, for I certainly had grown accustomed to his. From habit, I had adopted this stretch of dirt as my regular route into and out of the city. Mostly, I traversed it by foot (which takes longer than hailing a taxi, but I get to see more). Moreover, it allows me to bypass the military checkpoint at the off-ramp of the highway, an obstacle that obliges all motorists to a minimal two-hour wait before entering the city. So, with every passage on the foot road, I'd been finding the boy at this spot—a sandy, somewhat desolate patch of high ground. I reached it just yards after passing the rusted sign that bears the word "Hero," complete with a large, imposing arrow to point me in the right direction. But it has been the boy who actually leads me, his appearance the true announcement that I have entered the city's borders.

This is useful because Hero—with its quasi-stateless form of statehood—maintains borders which are sketchy, at best. This is particularly true at the western margin, where all of its hotels are (there being a grand total of three). The paucity of accommodations for visitors may be traced to the fact that the natives here see so few. The simple fact is, Hero is not any easy place to get to. My own trip involved nearly every method of locomotion known to man—plane, ship, helicopter, ferry, and finally, a bus; although it helps to bear in mind that my travel agent was Pea Nuts.

Logistics aside, the stone thrower is, without a doubt, my strongest image of Hero. But first, there is the paradoxical geography of his land. Hero is both no place and every place man has been. To sweep one's eyes across its dips and rises is to call up, instantly, the boy who casts the stone. The reason for this is practical, rather than poetic. The simple fact is that anyone who has ever been a child in Hero has, at one time or another, thrown a stone. It is a matter of civic pride, and one that (some say) grows straight from Hero's roots in ancient history—reputed to predate the floods.

There has almost never been a time that foreigners were not either contemplating, or actively invading, this small region that is at once a village, a primitive city, and an improvised nation. Heroaens readily point out that as long as there have been invasions, there has been resistance. This legacy of resistance has, throughout the ages, engendered a tremendous sense of power here. And yet, it is not the power of the mighty, but of the beleaguered. The greatest (indeed, only) weapon Heroaens are known to possess is their will. This leads me to describe them as a simple people—meaning only that they love things simple—while despising anything easy. Detesting technological advances, they cling to the view that modernity is, at best, a gimmick to impress the unsuspecting, and at worst, a lie. I have sometimes wondered whether Heroaens truly fight occupying armies, or whether they are simply fighting change. In the end, theirs may be defiance for its own sake. Having neither developed (nor aspired to) a modern army, nor sophisticated weaponry, such defiance finds natural expression in the stones. Its message is as simple as it is clear—Heroaens wish only to be left alone.

In spite of this, the conquerors come. Exactly what attracts them is perplexing, because Hero has neither strategic nor economic importance to any place other than itself. Yet Hero's significance, or its place in history, is not discernible on the surface. It takes some digging. It may well be impenetrable. Nevertheless, I am tempted to believe that it is the very stoicism of Heroaens, their fierce and famous will, that itself becomes the challenge. This, in the end, may be Hero's greatest appeal— to detractors and admirers alike.

And of course, there is the land. Nestled inward from the sea (no one has ever thought to measure the exact distance, though it is far), Hero is a harmony of opposites. Inland, it is an oasis of fertile hills, natural springs, and sprawling groves of olive and coffee. Radiating outward, however, is the geographical curiosity of sand. In describing the marvel, an ancient poet once proclaimed that "Hero is surrounded by desert—even as oceans caress its coasts on either side." As for the inhabitants, it may be due to the peculiar character of the early Heroaens that, rather than settling the fertile plains, they chose to build their homes on the desert side—drawn there, I guess, by its desolate beauty. Today, excavations continue to unearth artifacts of the original settlements buried deep below what is now known as Old City, or the popular term, "Old Hero."

From the dirt path, I reached a stretch of pavement that, while broken in places, might nonetheless be described as street. At once, I was faced with the immense iron arch which serves as symbolic, if not official, gateway to Old Hero. I passed under it, miraculously without having to be filtered through a military checkpoint. Within minutes of my entry, I was approached by the venerable and familiar coffee vendor. In a habit inspired by the locals, I immediately reached into my pack to produce the tin cup carried expressly for this purpose. For a coin and the exchange of an amicable "good morning," the vendor poured me the day's first dose of potent, steaming coffee from a large canister strapped to his back. Roving vendors are common on the streets of Old Hero, peddling everything from traditional sweets to pocket watches.

In the absence of a bench or outdoor table, I located a rock to sit on while sipping the coffee. It was more of a boulder, really. In terms of the vast geological matter of Hero, this particular piece had quickly become my pick. More than just a quirky habit, my sessions on The Rock are something of a ritual— an opportunity to collect my thoughts, reflect on potential connections, as well as gather the focus and momentum of my mission. Most importantly, this means consulting The List, my low-tech organizer of places-to-go-people-to-see. Salvaging it from the chaos of assorted note pads, water bottle, spare pens, and day-old peanut butter sandwiches tossed into my backpack,

I danced my eyes over the scribbled entries, line by line, pointing me towards an unfolding labyrinth of destinations.

FLEET OF KITES

Transportation in Hero is odious, even on a good day. From the arching gateway, I'd made the miscalculation of hailing the taxi that, true to form, got stuck in traffic. It sped the final three blocks, managing to deposit me in front of the morgue just as the tail lights of a shiny black van were pulling away. A witness informed me that it had curtailed yet another demonstrator—charged with making provocative gestures at police. Too bad I missed that one, too. In the wake of the arrest, I discovered the site in a state of relative, if deceptive, calm. Subjected to a head count, however, the few stragglers I'd seen two days ago proved to have added to their number. Many now carried handmade signs resembling a fleet of rickety kites.

It was mid-morning of the ninth day of protests, and I did not predict that getting *into* the morgue would be the formidable challenge. Gone was my idea that I could simply flash my journalist's credentials in order to be waved past the gate. The former uniformed watchman had been supplanted by a pair of burly guards. Pistols poked out of their belts alongside the spillover of bellies. But while their physiques belied the apathy of men listed on the government payroll, their faces were true to the role. They had the blank expressions of battle-scarred sentinels. Latently threatening, their cool eyes scanned the movements of the demonstrators whose number continued to expand by the minute. By noon, the guards were reinforced by a unit of soldiers who speedily fanned out amidst the crowd.

By mid-afternoon, the preoccupation of our collected humanity was to locate some shade from the stifling heat. Most sought relief by pressing in along the sidewalk, where the more resourceful began to erect paper tents out of their protest signs. Rapidly, the morning's fleet of rickety kites dissolved to a sort of tent city. While this offered some relief from the heat, it did little to ward off the flies. Protesters wrapped their heads in damp shirts to shield their ears from the intensity of the buzzing.

Surveying the scene, the exasperation of one of the guards was finally beginning to show. "You see this?" he exclaimed. "We will be neck deep in the soot and the ashes." As the crowd pressed in, we watched the street transform. What mere hours ago had been an empty expanse was now a suffocating swell of the masses. Neither I, nor the guard, could any longer see ten feet in front of us.

To recover my bearings, I decided to wade through the hoard in search of the familiar tree. It's funny how in Hero, where there is no ocean, the crowd swell fills in nicely for an incoming tide. Like a scientist, I think I have identified a landlocked form of seasickness. Under that condition, the tree would make a serviceable anchor. In addition, I was hoping to benefit from any shade it could offer. So, wasting no more time, I set out. Covering the short distance from the gate to the tree, however, required a roundabout navigation. Adrift along the sidewalk, I found myself swimming through the flotilla of kites as through the carnage of a ship wreck. Plundered bodies, floating on the ripples, swayed themselves dizzy with singed and broken mastheads.

In the ocean, too, I met my share of homeless sailors. They are easy to pick out of the crowd. I just look for the drab color of the soldier's uniform. Within minutes, I found one wearing the breast patch of an elite commando (bear in mind, of course, that the heat makes me see strange things). Lumbering, he seemed to assume the head of the bull before my eyes, but remained a man from the shoulders downward—from the feet back up to the tips of the fingernails. It is an informative transformation. The general of an army once told me (to my very real amazement) that "a man is a man because of his eyes and his hands," and that "without them, he is little above the station of the brute." But if the power isn't always the intelligent or effective brand, the mindless power of a brute has its force, too. In a war, this is the most devastating of all discoveries.

It may be common knowledge that every sailor has a story; it's true, too, of every soldier. And still, I am continually surprised at how much of it they willingly share with reporters like me. After noting my press ID card (more impressive to the sea bull than it had been to the guard at the gate), he, a soldier again, started to talk. "The crowd makes me nervous," he said. In a voice rupturing out in gurgles, his words resounded like the familiar verse of a song. At once, it recalled to me more than a decade of lightless days and sleepless nights, shared between men of like discomfort, and spread across every continent where there has been armed conflict. Throughout, I had collected story after story of soldiers' fears. Buried deep in the crypts of my note pad were the haunted records of memories recounted, over and over, of a single trigger-happy moment, when the twitch of a nerve resulted in the wounding of an innocent target. "But you see how it happens," one soldier maintained, "on days when even children take turns creeping up on us."

In the crowd that day, I passed scores of children. I did not find them particularly menacing; then again, maybe I just could not get past the vision of the rickety kites their parents had transformed to protest signs. I am not a soldier. But the sea bull is. Lowering his voice to a whisper, he made reluctant reference to an incident involving a girl. "We were searching a dark house with flashlights," he recalled, "when something dashed out of the shadows, fast and small. I couldn't think straight. But I was young then; it was my first time. In a flash, I discharged my weapon. It yelped, falling on four legs, limping away like a dog. The problem is, a child does not run as fast as a dog." Forcing a casual shrug, he added, "I was a little messed up after that." Concluding the recollection, Sea Bull turned and, in a wave, folded back into the foaming crowd.

I wandered some more, fed a cracker to a stray donkey, then squatted beside a soldier who'd picked an odd moment to dismantle and clean his weapon. I fed him question after question, while rapidly jotting down strings of words from the soldier's lexicon as he spewed them: the scope, the firing chamber, the barrel, the hollow-tip bullets—detailed terms describing the pieces of his rifle. He explained how, with the latest technology, laser lights mark the target. It struck me that color codes are important in this war. There are uniforms to distinguish good guys from bad guys, and a man's chest can be targeted by the master marksman with a laser beam of red. He applied the same cool analysis to matters of the psyche. "You may have heard that a soldier has dreams," he told me. "In mine, a blindfolded man stands in a field; his hands are bound. From behind him, another is looking and taking his picture—because it is a good photo moment. I have the feeling that the one with the camera is me.

"Later, as I look at the picture, I ask, 'what is the man thinking as he is about to die?' I decide that he is unaware, or indifferent, that his back is about to be shattered with lead. But how did I know, when I couldn't even see his eyes?" He looked at me with a puzzled expression. "To be soldiers, we understand that we are not entitled to live forever. But to meet the end with hands tied?" He shook his head, "This is, for me, the greatest terror." Then he rounded back to the enigma of the blindfolded man. "I do not understand why he is not more fearful or angry—unless, hours ago, he saw his fate. Maybe the man has already left his body. Behind the blindfold, the eyes would show this." With a sigh, he repeated the side-to-side motion with his head, apparently in the effort to shake off the man's—and his own—bewilderment. Nearby, the donkey snorted and flicked its tail to swat away a fly.

I continued, aimless, until arriving within sight of the tree I have come to recognize. At once, the vision struck me as an island oasis, and I the hapless sailor coming at last to shore. By then, the only element missing was the nymph. Fittingly, it was at that spot that *I first saw her* as a sallow girl making the protracted emission of a sigh. With hair unevenly cropped and partially subdued into pigtails, she had the wild look of a tiger with one ear slightly drooping—waking, perhaps, from an afternoon's lengthy nap. She paced in circles while I, straining with all my senses, did not pick up the slightest vibration.

SPICE AND SAUSAGE

In Hero, it's remarkable what may be accomplished for the passing of a fee. Locals call it the base cost of doing business and, when it works, I'm not one to argue. Just like a native, I may be more pragmatist than purist. Hero also teaches that a man can only be as honest as the system he has to work in. This is nowhere more true than at its prison. Having initially procured my way in by paying the warden, I hoped to apply a similar strategy with the inmate. More than anything, my first meeting with Hektor had convinced me that these walls, and the lives of those within them, contained everything I needed to look for in Hero—the face that, beneath the craggy skin's surface, is a dry well of plugged ducts and forgotten scars. Hero, sad and honest. I'd never met a man better able to express this than Hektor, but I knew that to obtain his story, I needed his trust. The solution to getting it was easy. I sought to bribe him.

Wary of a spate in negative publicity, the Prison Board had agreed to resolve the hunger strike as quickly as possible—and in the inmates' favor. In honor of that victory, I returned to the prison bearing a parcel of sausage concealed in newsprint paper. Attempting to squeeze it through the spaces of the bars, I was immediately caught by the guard on duty—who was the same man as the last time—and who confiscated the sausage. I wondered aloud to Hektor if the meat would make it back to the fat wife. Hektor shot a side glance at the portly guard and said, "I doubt it." For me, the lesson was amply clear. On my next visit, I presented the sausage in duplicate copy—one for Hektor, and one for the portly guard. So call it a fee if you want to, or call it the base cost of doing business in Hero. For myself, I call it no less than a small victory against the bureaucracy of the prison. Impressed with my own cleverness, I grew a little smug, at that. The next time I saw Hektor, I asked, "How did you like the sausage?" He replied plainly, "The cell guys say 'don't buy it so spicy next time.'" It occurred to me, belatedly, that everything in prison is shared.

Through trial and error, I would eventually learn to buy the sausages in the right degree of spice (and happily, would see them more than redeem their worth). Not only was the modest tribute helping me to earn the trust of Hektor, but from it, access to the vast, internal network otherwise impenetrable to outsiders—the Heroaen neighborhood.

"Keep in mind that I don't like reporters," Hektor warned me, "but I have an idea of what you're after." He paused to slip a cigarette between his teeth. "So, I've decided to help you."

"That's a gracious offer," I replied, "but it depends on your idea of what I'm 'after.'"

"You want to talk to people—martyrs' families, war victims, orphans, that kind of thing."

"Sounds ghoulish when you put it that way, but alright."

"Got a pencil?"

COFFEE WITH SOPHI

The apartment looked as if it had been molded from sand, then encased within walls of weather-worn yellow brick. In spite of the clear distress associated with age, the building maintained a battered dignity in the details. Windows were plentiful and generous, patterning the brick facade into an array of rows and columns. Balconies, wrought from iron, further divided the windows into individual apartments, setting them off with delicate black grills weaving an intricate balance of lines and circles. The more cheerful of the balconies were spotted with clay pots sprouting the thyme that families use for cooking. I am told that prior to the Great Uprising, many of these balconies would have been festooned with the bright red petals of geraniums—a favorite local flower. But, due to the ongoing economic sanctions, flowers had all but disappeared from Heroaen households. Almost all of the balconies, however, shared the feature of a permanent clothesline strung with laundry.

Entering the atrium of the building, I saw a cage containing the manually-operated elevator. Forgoing that, I took the stairs. At the third floor, I located the apartment number I'd watched Hektor laboriously scrawl into my note pad, then rapped my knuckles several times against the thick wood door. It opened to reveal a sleepy young lady who studied me with a mild curiosity. A half drank bowl of coffee was still cradled in her hand, infusing the entry space with its dense, bittersweet aroma.

"I am sorry to disturb your breakfast," I began, quickly explaining that I was a reporter pursuing a story. In the effort to appease her calm but skeptical expression, I immediately displayed my press identification card, which she perused with a demure glance. Attempting to further convince her, I flashed the morning's edition of The Chronicle which I'd been carrying rolled up under my arm.

The young lady smiled.

"It's no problem," she reassured me. "I am well aware of the paper. In fact, I've read a few of your stories."

"I am flattered," I replied.

"But I wonder," she continued, "why does the paper say, 'J.R. Teheda?' Why so many initials?"

"Oh that's just my *byline*," I answered—in newspeople terms. When the word caused her to raise an eyebrow, I felt additionally foolish. "A byline simply means the name of the author, which, in this case, is me."

"I understand that," she persisted, in all politeness. "But what I am really asking is, what does the 'J.R.' stand for?"

"My apologies," I offered, finally realizing the error of my clumsy introduction. "It's James. James Robert Teheda. But you can call me Teheda."

I detected the hint of a frown.

"Or James, if you prefer. Call me Robert, for that matter. Call me whichever you like."

"Alright, then. I'll call you James. I like James. Anyway, it's so much better than calling you by a surname, 'Teheda this,

Teheda that,'—as though we're in the army. Please, call me Sophi."

So this was Sophi. Her voice was every bit as sweet as the name.

"How can I help you?" she volunteered.

"By answering a few questions, if you don't mind."

She gestured me toward a small room past the kitchen.

"Perhaps we'd like to sit in the parlor," she suggested.

"By all means," I agreed, then followed her into the cramped space overstuffed with an abundance of chairs. Each item of furniture had the look of having been re-upholstered at least twice, and with fabrics that never quite matched. The effect, altogether, was a hodgepodge décor I've observed in a good number of Heroaen homes. Despite the clutter, such interiors do not lack charm; albeit, a frenetic, frazzled kind.

"Shall I prepare coffee?" the young lady asked.

It is rare, indeed, to be invited into a Heroaen household without this gesture of hospitality.

"I'd be grateful," I replied.

Sophi vanished into the kitchen. In her absence, I nosily studied the objects in the room. It was strewn, foremost, with intricate samples of embroidery in varying stages of completion. Hero is a nation of artisans; and, like the clutter, items of needlework can be found in almost every room. Against the far wall, I saw a rough, unvarnished table (probably hand-constructed), topped off with a porcelain water jug resting in an enormous basin. This, I've been told, is the Heroaen solution to a water shortage. Water in Hero is rationed by the municipal authority (operating in collusion with the occupying government); at times, it can be shut off without warning or, for that matter, explanation. Families have learned to store away a little extra.

A short distance beyond the table containing the water jug, a child-size chair had been placed against the wall. The chair itself was plain, and would have escaped my attention had it not been for the doll nestled in the seating. Attired in a festive lace-trimmed dress, she had the unmistakable aura of a bride—although a slightly forlorn one. This resulted, I think, from the permanently fixed position of her hands. The thumbs and fingers formed a circle—as in anticipation of holding a bouquet. But for this doll, the flowers were missing.

Momentarily, I began to hear the tinny clanking of utensils, the sliding of drawers, and the soft, faint brushing of Sophi's sandals against the wooden panels of the floor in the kitchen. These sounds were joined by those of pounding—no doubt my hostess crushing beans into powder with a mortar and pestle. Soon, the air became imbued with a palpable scent—the biting perfume of coffee. It mingled perfectly with the aroma of bread just then baking in the oven. With deliberate effort, I shook off that momentary (although pleasant) distraction of the senses, and returned my attention to the parlor.

On second glance, I managed to identify among the clutter assorted piles of books and newspapers. Among these were at least a few copies of The Chronicle, nearly lost among the more prevalent novels and comics.

Finally, my visual tour of the parlor culminated in what should have been the obvious. Clearly the most prominent feature in the room, it had managed, bizarrely, to escape my notice. There is an adage that you are least likely to see that which you are looking for. In my line of work, I have found this often to be true. Set inside an ornate frame, the handsome face of a young man stared out from a photograph. It was arranged on a high table and augmented by candles—the altar to a martyr, revering the passing of a loved one. No self-respecting Heroaen family seems to lack this feature, and I guess I shouldn't have been surprised. Hektor had promised me a martyr family. And he wasn't kidding.

Sophi reappeared carrying a tray. Gingerly setting it down, she transferred a plate of bread along with a pair of thimble-size ceramic cups to a low table in front of me. With remarkable grace, she tipped the spout of the brass boiler, filling mine first, carefully floating the top with a delicate layer of foam. Filling her own cup, she said, "Now then, what was it you wanted to ask me?"

Displaying uncharacteristic restraint, I decided not to ask about the altar. Instead, we began by discussing the riots and the weather, moving inexorably towards the topic of the late Commander (after all, his was the story I had come for). Of him, I obtained the following description:

"He was a little rough, usually unshaven," Sophi recalled, "but still, a most good-looking man. He had those very sad eyes. They were full of resolve."

She paused, watching with interest as I jotted my notes into a journal. When the novelty of observing me faded, Sophi began tapping the tips of her fingers against the porcelain sides of her cup, but hesitated to continue. I prompted.

"Are you aware what the Commander might have done for a living?"

"He called himself a 'craftsman'—very proud of the hundred years that his family made soap. It's funny that to us young people, he was a legend for all he did in the war. But on meeting him, I was a little disappointed. All he ever talked about was soap."

For more than a century, the Commander's family ran the local factory (a building that, remarkably, dates back an additional two thousand years). At the outbreak of GU-1 in the recent decade, the heir returned from prison to discover that his inheritance had been annexed by the state as a defensive measure against rebels (both existing and prospective). The seizure policy—regarded as illegal by international law—is but one more legacy of the Great Uprising.

Stepping out to the balcony, Sophi and I were afforded a remarkable view of the edifice that, proclaimed an historical treasure, today sits abandoned and inactive. In its medieval past, Hero was dotted with factories very much like this one, making it Soap Central of its corner of the world. But by now the ancient manufacture of soap has been supplanted by mass production, pushing the handmade product to the verge of extinction. As for the traditional buildings where soap had been turned out for centuries, a large number were gutted for commercial or municipal functions; others demolished outright. Today, only the Commander's factory survives in its original, if non-operational, form. "He talked about reviving the business," Sophi recalled, "'when peace comes.' Then those sad eyes of his took on a light, almost happy expression. My sister really fell for that. After all, she was impressionable."

Without much effort, perhaps even without intention, the Commander beguiled Antigone with descriptions of soap.

Antigone.

I wondered how my list from Hektor could have left out such an unforgettable name. Before taking my leave of Sophi, I inquired into the possibility of making her sister's acquaintance.

"One of these days, who knows?"

Sophi left me to make what I would of that enigmatic reply.

CHAPTER THREE

DESTINATIONS

COOLER

OLD CITY, Hero — In the days ahead, I discovered that I'd already taken—or stolen—my first glimpse of Antigone by the foot of the tree opposite the morgue. If, alternately, I had spotted her at the park, or at the market, or at any tree but that one, then destiny might just as well have taken a detour. In the configuration of events, of course, beside the tree was where I saw her. What I'd noticed, moreover, was just how tiny she was, as Sophi said, "a very small slip of a girl."

Tiny and perhaps, again in the words of her sister, "invisible." Surely, that's how the girls felt when, one far afternoon in Sophi's memory, they sat side by side in fold-up chairs at one end of the family parlor. It would have been the very location where I observed the altar; because from that day forward, the chairs would be set aside to make room for a table. Upon it would be set the image of an icon—a revered, if somewhat transformed, representation of a brother still very much alive in memory.

Across from them had stood the enormous cooler belonging to the florist, which had been borrowed and situated in the center of the room as part of a vigil no one had taken the time to explain to them. Antigone kicked her foot against the cheap metal frame of the chair, looking obliquely upward. She might have expected to be scolded, as she repeatedly had been for the past two hours for every instance of kicking the chair, or moving a finger, or sneezing. But she wasn't. She was no longer being noticed, not by anyone, not even by the unmoving guardian posted beside her for reasons no one had explained.

"I want to go outside," Antigone whispered.

Sophi folded her arms and did not look down.

Antigone turned her eyes to the glass pane at the opposite wall of the parlor, which, in the smothering heat, remained fixed to its frame at each of the edges. But when she asked, "Can't we open the window?" Sophi had looked down at her for an instant and curled her lips into a firm-yet-subtle frown. Antigone murmured, "It's just that I think I'm choking." Inhaling meant drawing in particles of ash. And yet, in the room suffused with an odor she could not identify, large parties of people came and went, no one commenting on the closure of the windows.

Nowhere in that mix could Antigone detect the scent of flowers, because there were none. The cooler, donated by the man who once earned a living in roses, today contained something else that Antigone had been told not to look at, even though other people did nothing but look.

FROM THE FIRST morning Sophi opened her door to me, I'd been falling under the spell of her voice. Like the distant song of a mermaid, it has the power to lead dolphin armies and part oceans at will. Yet, in spite of that otherworldly, sonic quality, I've now figured out that the magic is only partly physical. It has as much to do with what she's saying as how she says it. Because like a good Heroaen, Sophi cares most about telling the truth.

"What do you want to know about my brother?" she began. "That he ranked first in his class, regardless of performance? That he was valedictorian—the first guy classmates turn out to vote for; the captain of the team; the champion of sports both ancient and yet-to-be-invented? Is that what you want to know?"

"That, and whatever else you'd like to tell me," I suggested.

"I can tell you that everybody loved him, and why not? Imagine the guy who is never shy of confidence when called upon to speak in front of a crowd; and never fails to deliver the impressive speech that, on closer inspection, says nothing. Then picture a boy whose perfect teeth flash blinding smiles— brightening a face that grows more handsome with each day of neglect. If you can picture this, you have all that I ever knew of my brother. That is as much as I can say about him," Sophi concluded, and with a trace of sadness, "I don't know what more there is, except, maybe, that he measured the value of life by degrees of danger, even if it meant looking everywhere to find it. And he did—in all the predictable places. When he ran out of those, he found there was still one thing missing. At nineteen, Tibolt wasn't yet a hero. So, one day he sped his car through the border to defy the guards. He had no weapon. Any more questions?"

ON THAT DISTANT MORNING, Antigone asked a few.

"Why do the windows have to be closed? Where is mother?... Why is Tibolt inside the cooler?" and, for the hundredth time, "Why can't we go outside?"

Sophi had managed to ignore her, until finally Antigone asked, "Is he cold?"

Sophi said, "Probably."

It was then that it occurred to Antigone that she knew why Tibolt was in the cooler. He was there because he wanted to sleep with the flowers, just like on the morning he'd come into the parlor smelling of flowers, like he had slept in them. And there was grass in his hair, and the smell of the soil...

Sophi laughed, without derision, perhaps, but not without a hint of meanness. "If he smelled of flowers," she said, "it must have been her perfume. He is always running around with the lady who smells of perfume."

"Which lady?"

"It doesn't matter. One of them."

No one Antigone knew ever wore perfume, which she guessed must smell something like flowers. There were no flowers in Hero, not now. And if there had not been flowers in Hero for a long time, she could see why Tibolt's lady would wear perfume, to remind her of flowers where there were none. Tibolt must have found out for himself when he got into the cooler. There are no flowers. And what if he is alone in there?

"Is there a lady smell inside the cooler with Tibolt?" Antigone asked, this time getting a sigh for an answer. Sophi was tired of questions and wouldn't talk anymore. Antigone slumped back into her chair. People were coming into the room and acting like shadows. Some had curled-down mouths and wrinkles in the tops of their faces, above the eyebrows. The women walked over to the chairs, saying words to Sophi to make her nod and answer the way mother had taught them to speak to adults. Then the women would look a long time at Antigone, kneel down to wipe the dark, uneven strands of hair that were sticking to her forehead. And still, no one would open the window.

Then, in a commotion of wailing from the chorus of women, a number of men entered the room.

"At last," Sophi said, her voice making the crackle of blue rocks under the soles of people's sandals. "They have come for Tibolt."

As they lifted him out of the cooler, Antigone was surprised to see how small he was, as if the cold had shrunk him. The shadows of the women followed those of the men as they carried Tibolt, on his back so as not to wake him, in the direction of the doorway. Disappearing through it, the wailing grew louder, piercing the powdery air.

"He is going away," Sophi explained.

"Where?"

"I'm not sure, but some place far."

"When he gets there, will he have flowers?"

"No," Sophi stated sternly. "In Hero there are no flowers."

It wasn't true though.

"Sophi, make them wait," Antigone pleaded.

"I can't," Sophi answered. "It's time for us to follow. Get up now."

She lifted Antigone by the arm, pulling her from the chair and pushing her forward toward the doorway. Reaching it, Antigone could see down the length of the corridor, where the men were still carrying Tibolt on his back so as not to wake him. And the wailing of the women grew louder.

Antigone wrenched her arm free of the grip of Sophi. Running to the bedroom, she picked up her doll that was sitting on the bed, resting against the fatness of the pillow.

"For Tibolt," Antigone explained, gently freeing the bouquet from the bride's cradling arms. But without Tibolt to put his nose to them and say, "Mmm, how pretty," the flowers did not smell like anything. "It's because they are made of plastic," Sophi had explained. "They're not even real."

That wasn't true, either, because they had been real enough to Tibolt. On the morning he came home from the fields, smelling like the soil and the perfume lady, he had staggered like a clown, giddy, walking in on Antigone as she was setting up the altar for a wedding.

"And this, the lovely bride?" he noted, picking up the doll propped up beside the altar. She was holding her flowers. It was then that he'd buried his nose in the bouquet and said, "Mmm, how pretty." After that, he'd sprawled out beside the altar and, as he often did, passed out on the floor of the parlor. In a short while, he had begun to snore.

"Sophi, make them wait!" Antigone pleaded, though Sophi was too far ahead to hear her. She was walking close behind the wailing women, who trailed the men, who were carrying Tibolt on his back so as not to wake him. By now, the procession had gone down into the street. Antigone ran, with feet pinched by the straps of her sandals, and with hands clasping the bouquet of flowers that Sophi had said were nothing but plastic.

FILE CABINET

Once again, an off-the-record transaction gained me access to territory otherwise off-limits. Too bad an extra figure had to be tagged onto the price, the morgue director said, to assure that my access to his vault remain "exclusive." He drove a tough bargain, indeed. I had the unbearable lightness of my pockets to prove it. Newly paupered, I yet held to the conviction that what might be glimpsed inside was priceless beyond measure, certainly beyond what could be entered into the ledger.

On the inside, the morgue contained wall-to-wall stacks of refrigerated compartments, neatly lined and labeled like the drawers of a file cabinet. There is an enormous room just like it at The Chronicle, and we call it The Archive. Drawers of The Archive are stuffed with records, digitally burned into permanence until the next office fire. In the morgue, too, the drawers contain histories and records. Predating digital technology, they are the stuff of human memory and matter— all recently expired, and whose impermanence is guaranteed. Yet, it is an archive of sorts. Convincingly, the drawers feature slips of cardboard indicating identifying numbers, like toe tags. And, like the drawer's contents, the label is temporary— removable by lifting the cardboard tag out of its metal frame and replacing it with another. I'm sure the Commander himself had been assigned one, although I had not the time, or didn't think to, record it into my notebook. The serial number, like the man, proved yet another form of impermanence.

MASKED

From a slide-out slab of the refrigerated drawer, the lab assistant pealed back the plastic sheeting to reveal a face disfigured with the bruises of death. Only later on, after rescuing much of the man's story from communal memory, did I realize that I, myself, had known him. Our acquaintance had been casual; in summary, a single meeting. But it was enough to allow me to recall a familiarity. It was not a matter of remembering the face—neither for its scale or ferocity, the emphatic eyebrows, nor the near permanent presence of stubble. I might have recognized him by the eyes, described by many as his most distinguishing feature, but they had not been open.

The fact is that at the time I met him, the Commander had drawn a black knit hood over his head. Two cutouts above the nose provided his only windows, his frontier for interaction with the world. "Informants are everywhere," he stated, the words escaping through a third slit accommodating his mouth. "We take precautions." His implication, short of suspicion, was not directed at myself, but rather at the lens of the photographer's camera. Its purpose was to capture and broadcast his image to new stands locally and across continents. He had every reason to worry. It is not difficult to understand why, for hunted men, masks are vitally important. By the strangest contrast, the armed man who had accompanied the Commander—virtually as his shadow—did not appear to share the apprehension. With face exposed but barely noticed, the gunman had simply assumed his station at the sill of the window, where he remained.

Overall, the Commander impressed me as a young leader whose experience had aged him beyond his years. The sturdy build and steady voice notwithstanding, he seemed cloaked in the aura of an old man. The eyes, while underlined by dark circles and somewhat droopy, were indeed full of resolve—just as Sophi had described them. Their fatigue, moreover, attested to the challenges of his occupation and its peculiar brand of success. If being top rebel meant catching short sleep on floors borrowed on the benevolence of strangers, it was but one of the joys accompanying his local celebrity. He introduced himself by a nom de guerre which, translated in the rough, can be taken as a synonym for his city—Hero. A more nuanced interpretation yields, "he who strives against himself to serve."

We met in a secluded, sparsely furnished apartment. In spite of the informality, indeed secrecy, of the gathering, Hero was unfailingly polite, pouring each of us a thimble-size cup of syrupy coffee to accompany pastries parceled out on paper plates. Toasted layers of wheat sprinkled over cheese and dripping golden honey, it was the regional specialty— and a delicacy for which this city is famous. "Please," he said, pushing the plates toward us, "enjoy." Accepting my portion, I made the observation foreigners often do. This is a land of unbridled hospitality. A colleague of mine once suggested that if kidnapped, at least he could count on being well fed.

"Everybody comfortable?" my host asked jokingly. "Good. Then let's proceed." For the next hour, we discussed factional politics, glossing over details that he did not want printed. At the time, I hardly predicted that my interview with the masked rebel would result in the most acclaimed article I would write that year (The Chronicle named it "Best International Feature"). The fact was that I hadn't even initiated the meeting. He had. And when I'd responded skeptically to the invitation, he explained, rather directly, that he wanted publicity. What's more, he said he'd been following my byline "from war-to-war." Though it surprised me to learn that I had a fan club, the explanation reflected the growing tendency in rebel leadership to view their struggles as universal. In business terms, this meant taking advantage of the multi-national pool of publicity talent. What it suggested in local terms was that the competing rebel factions were paying increasing attention to public relations—to putting a positive spin on the stories that reached the international press in hopes of generating sympathy for their cause. It is a campaign I am tempted to dub "Even Militants Are People." More and more, the rebels were adopting corporate strategies, perhaps finally accepting that it is a corporate war, and not very romantic at all.

I'd certainly met his brand of rebel leader before. They are discreet, charismatic—and alpha to the core. But in the case of "Hero," a soft-spoken modesty all but defied the role. I had the impression of a man who, if given the choice, might have preferred to lead without calling attention to himself.

As dictated by local courtesy, I savored my coffee down to the grinds. Then, closing my note pad, I announced my confidence that the information he provided would make a good story, and that I would try to have it ready for the upcoming Special Features edition. He thanked me, but added, "If you don't mind my asking, what is your name?"

If it was his turn to be curious about me, that's only fair. Still, the question was puzzling. All readers of The Chronicle may recognize my byline as J. R. Teheda. Did he suspect me of using a pseudonym (the reporter's version of a nom de guerre)? Then again, I am in a part of the world where the hiding of one's identity is not a mere matter of discretion. It is a matter of survival.

RIVALS

"Some day," Luis declared, "I'm going to beat you to the headline, Teheda. Your corpse story made nice front page splash."

It had been published as a Chronicle Exclusive—which Luis would no doubt be holding against me. He wrote for its tabloid competitor, The Daily Cosmos.

"Still paying your sources?"

"Do you know a better way?"

"Do you know that you're in Hero?" he scoffed. "It's a matter of not getting fleeced on the price. Folks here know how to turn a deal." Luis' own dejection was apparent, likely from himself having overlooked the morgue as a bribe-worthy venue. Otherwise, he might well have out-bid me.

Luis worked Hero's system of para-economics as well as anyone—a fact I gleaned three years ago from our lengthy (often accidental) conversations at the bar. Of the ninety-three days I'd then spent in Hero, about ninety-two evenings had wound down at Zax. Leaving the bureau office, I'd scout for dinner at midnight—the hour when tired reporters put aside rivalries to seek rare moments of camaraderie. On those occasions, Luis and I had struck up an easy, if tenuous, friendship. In spite of that, an underlying tension remains. It traces back to the wide impression that The Daily Cosmos, Luis' employer, might more accurately be titled "The Daily Gossip." The Cosmos displays a flare for unsubstantiated and lurid events, and to the dismay of serious journalists everywhere, is also Hero's most widely read paper—more proof that sensationalism sells.

This time, I had apparently out-done the sensationalists with my morgue exclusive. Morbid and surreal, it captured the imagination of the public in a way that The Cosmos, with all its efforts, had failed to. For Luis, this was the very reason it rankled. Morgue story aside, Luis is less than proud of his association with the tabloid. "Personally, I read The Chronicle," he confessed.

APOCALYPSE

The assassination of the rebel commander occurred minutes before midnight, just days before I was called back to Hero. After the shock of the killing, news of it had coursed like wildfire through the streets—without the customary assistance of the press. Like a spontaneous, organic outbreak, it was simply whispered from household-to-household by the city's insomniacs. Among that number had been the municipal governor, so that by the sixth hour of morning, an urgent meeting of his officials was convening in his kitchen. While a transcript of that session is unlikely to surface, I afterwards learned from the governor that it amounted to "a babble—we talked of nothing but the Great Uprising." It's no surprise that GU continued to haunt a generation of governors. Some vividly recalled the public stonings of their colleagues accompanied by

the burning of their houses—"Hero razed by its own citizens,"
the governor spat in a fit of disgust. In his kitchen that more
recent morning, the officials determined to avert another cycle
of violence by subverting any opportunity for the public to
gather. In practical terms, this meant stamping the Commander
an Enemy of the State—thereby rendering, by ancient law, the
illegality of his funeral.

Days after viewing his body at the morgue, it was with a
blank disbelief that I found out about the prohibition of the
Commander's funeral the same way everybody else did—by
reading about it in the afternoon edition of The Daily Cosmos.
Accosting me in the street in front of Zax, Luis presented me
with an unrolled copy.

"This one's for you, Teheda, straight off the press. The ink's
not dry yet."

Across the front page splashed the official pronouncement.

"They've declared the prohibition of a funeral," I said,
incredulous. "What century are we in? How the hell…"

"The Governors' Council held a closed door meeting," Luis
disclosed. "I found out by an inside contact."

He had finally beaten me to the headline.

Although congratulations were in order, they became
drowned out by the shouts of crowds emptying the coffee shops
and surging into the streets. Copies of The Cosmos were then
coming off the trucks, beginning to pass from hand to hand—
like bacterial contagion. As news spread additionally from
mouth-to-mouth, The Cosmos was increasingly abandoned.
Loose sheets of it were left to blow along the pavements, where
it clung like fly paper to the soles of shoes.

Somewhere in the flood, I lost Luis. On my own then, I
advanced toward the driver of an idling taxi, folded myself into
the passenger cabin, and abruptly slammed the door.

"I need to get to the morgue," I declared, "*in a hurry*."

"Sir, if that's your pleasure," a droll voice replied, with no
visible movement of the head.

Every cab driver in Hero is sarcastic. But I was lucky this
time. The talking head proved himself an impeccable driver,

managing to weave us through the otherwise static lanes. Speechless, I spent the initial mile gazing out the cabin window, marveling at sights that ranged from grim to delightful—and too often, side-by-side. No matter how many times I have passed these streets, the feeling persists that they are unfolding for the very first time. At ground level, they are battered and crumbling, smothered with a pallor of decay. And yet, even at a glance, there is exuberance and vitality between the cracks. Beneath it all is a motley foundation of gray.

I was still viewing my driver's head from the back side when I decided to ask, "Is Hero always this pretty?" He replied, "Only when it's under siege." Without prompting, he launched a tirade against the imperialist occupiers of his country, while reserving the best of his ire for their native-born cohorts. "The foreigners are dogs, and their collaborators are the stuff dogs leave in the street."

Needless to say, Hero is lax about enforcing its scooper laws, if, indeed, it has any.

"I'd like to boil the whole lot of them in a vat of coffee. And after the grinds turn a sickly color, I will throw all of it to the dogs."

At my request for permission to quote him, his diatribe got even more interesting.

"I ask that you not print my words," he stated, "because with them, I have committed an injustice. I have insulted the dogs." Momentarily, he ground our vehicle to a halt in front of the walkway leading to the familiar iron gate. "Hero Morgue," he announced, his voice assuming the decorum of a sea captain. "You asked for pretty? You got it. Right through those gates, my friend."

There were no guards at the entrance, and not much else that had not been trampled. Minutes earlier, the mob had made its bull run against the morgue's bolted doors, and I had missed the action—again. Advancing to the vault, I saw only what the frenzied citizens had left in their wake—corpses pulled from the drawers of their refrigerated compartments, and turned unceremoniously out onto the floor. To the chagrin of the masses, none had been that of the Commander. Moreover, as the spilled cadavers had begun to thaw, the floor took on the sticky sheen of a dirty sidewalk after rain. So, like the earlier sheets of newsprint, the dislodged pieces of cardboard—body tags—stuck to the soles of my shoes.

PART 11

FACTORY

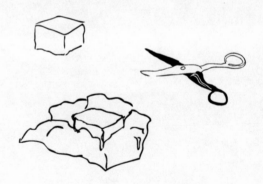

CHAPTER FOUR

HALLOWED GROUNDS

NAVIGATION

WEST SIDE, Hero — Its initial bust jolted me up from the hotel bed where, paralytically, I did nothing but glare at the alarm. The fact that it looked like a clock only disguised its more specific function of a human timer (the only question being, was I done yet?). Like a twelve-minute egg, hard-boiled would be just about right. I may even have felt a few degrees overcooked—which luckily did not impair my balance. Having struck a perfect right angle, I more-or-less chose to remain (if stasis is a kind of choice). My eyes then dropped straight shut—for keeps, it seemed—at least until the next audio attack (which launch intermittently). Out of habit, I let the timer continue for the next half hour on the unremitting setting labelled "Snooze"—a cruel misnomer. It's more of a sustained assault on the auricular sensors. At the end of the self-allotted thirty-so minutes, I managed to silence the buzzer by frantically punching an array of buttons (a real feat since my eyes were closed).

I fell back against the saggy mattress where, motionless, I soaked in the pre-dawn light of the tiny hotel room. I began to dream, with calculated precision, the many ways I might save Hero from itself—but they all required getting out of bed. I then wondered whether I had really slept at all, or simply passed the night in an opaque, insomniac fog. Either way, I'd traversed the hours to arrive at yet another begin-the-day in Hero. Considering the morning's agenda, I came up with a list of tasks, though none of them inspired me profoundly. First, I would attempt some connectivity with the world. In most respects, I am a solitary man. Still, I admit to those areas in life where a man cannot exist alone, and those times when "alone" borders on the unbearable. Mornings are a fine example. Fishing among the folds of the sheets, I located my steady companion—the perky cell phone with the colorful buttons (that will even sing me to sleep if asked to). My first call of the day was to the weather forecasting service. Cheerfully, a recorded voice greeted me, informed me whether to expect rain, draught, tempest or any manner of cosmological disruption, alerted me to the pollen count, and wished me a nice day. I chose a fresh shirt from among the row of identical others staring up at me from the flung open lid of my suitcase. Dressed and groggy, I proceeded to the hunt for a thoroughly potent cup of coffee. In Hero, this involves no more difficulty than stepping from the hotel out into the street, where coffee peddlers are as omnipresent as the pebbles.

I navigated my way to the press office which, in the three years since I'd been there, hadn't changed one bit (Pea Nuts informs me that not even the rent has gone up). By 7 A.M., I began reviewing the dispatches that would determine the course of my day—a virtual ticker tape account of events known to have transpired over the hours that I was supposed to be sleeping. I encountered the usual lineup of riot activity: street protest resulting in clash of civilians with military authorities, twelve wounded; shootout in one of the precincts, two dead, six wounded; crude rocket launched toward imperial magistrate's building, property damage with no wounded. I noted, with cultivated detachment, the low death count. A slow night. Sickly, I found myself hungering for something as ordinary as a robbery or mugging. I yearned for something as simple as a crime.

I managed to find it in a sentence drifting across my computer screen. It was so quick, my eyes nearly missed it; but I was curious, and decided to give it a second pass. It said, "Custodian of municipal cemetery reports missing body; current whereabouts unknown." The notation was dated last night, 1 AM, the approximate time that, exhausted, I had rolled into bed. Again, it might have been the overwrought brain juiced up on caffeine, but I could not let this go. Who would remove a body, and why? And what, if anything, had this to do with the Commander? An investigation played out prematurely in my head. The authorities would provide, at best, some stingy information: the deceased person's age, time and cause of death, short list of vital statistics, and if I was lucky, a name—clues that merely hint at a story. At worst, I might not even get that.

On this day, it was the worst case scenario that won out. My first informant in the case was the municipal magistrate's assistant, who, due to budgetary cutbacks, was filling the dual role of cemetery director. He refused, first off, to provide his own name, much less the name of the deceased person, and only after sustained grilling was I able to pull from him the following account. It began with my attempt to confirm the little information I had gathered from the wire service dispatch.

"At approximately midnight, a body was exhumed from one of the plots here. Is that correct?" I asked.

"Well, not exactly."

I raised an eyebrow. The assistant cleared his throat.

"It is more accurate to say that it was around midnight that the body was discovered missing."

"Discovered by whom?"

"The grounds keeper on the night shift."

Interestingly, he did not volunteer the custodian's name. I inquired it, along with the possibility of meeting the fellow directly.

"I'd like to accommodate you," the magistrate's assistant responded. "However, our maintenance crew is extensive. To track down the name of the individual is no simple matter. You have no idea of the mountains of papers, the time sheets, memos regarding changes to the schedule caused by vacations and sick days. To compound things, I am expected nowadays to operate without a secretary. Cutbacks, they've affected the municipalities, you know?"

"Hard times for everyone," I concurred. "However, I'd like to make it worth your effort. In consideration of your staffing shortage, of course, there'll be no need for a receipt. Extra paper work, you know?"

In Hero, this is the secret language of negotiating a fee—off the record.

After reaching some form of agreement in the monetary figure, the assistant grew a great deal more cooperative, and I was able to procure from him some additional details.

"Very well then," I announced, "may we proceed to the scene of the crime?"

IT IS SAID IN HERO that death is a liberation from life and its material trappings; this extols, I think, the impossibility of taking our wealth or status with us into the afterlife, and that there is equality in returning to the dust. However, one needs only to study the municipal cemetery to realize that this is hardly the case. An egalitarian utopia it is not. As we set out from the magistrate's assistant's office, I noted, initially, the acres of grassy, manicured plots. Many were marked by sculpted headstones that stood as lasting monuments to the wealthier citizenry, whether of Heroaen origin or foreign import. Most of these, as I learned from reading the elaborate inscriptions, were the deceased members of prominent families with connections to the imperial elite. As we turned down a remote path, however, I noted the gradual deterioration of the grounds. Mowed grasses gave way to stretches of gravel and eventually, to naked dirt. Without a single sign to announce it, I understood that we were passing into a separate section, reserved, apparently, for the city's underclass. Not surprisingly, the majority of headstones bore identifying inscriptions that were recognizably native, but the grave we arrived at had conspicuously been left unmarked. Standing at the rim of the long—but shallow—dugout, I sunk with the realization that I was not merely searching for a body. In Hero, as much as elsewhere, every body owes its identity to a name.

In this case, it was the most important thing missing.

GROUNDS KEEPER

Later in the day, I decided to give the cemetery an additional look—this time without the magistrate's assistant. If discovered, I planned on feigning innocence. After all, who needs official permission to visit a cemetery? Still, the last thing I needed was to be seen sniffing around. The assistant, tight-lipped and edgy, would hardly welcome my presence for a second round. I had the further motive of tracking down the grounds keeper who'd been on duty the night the unknown body was removed from its plot. My off-the-record transaction with the assistant had yielded the custodian's name, along with curt description of him as "a slim, sinewy man with suntanned skin and hollow bones. He'll be the one with the shovel"—which just about covers every farmer or landscaper in Hero.

I looked for Hollow Bones in the usual places—the staff office (the hut); the vending machines, the locker rooms, the equipment checkout station, staging areas along the trails that weave throughout the sprawling cemetery. Failing to find him in any, I proceeded to the most obvious spot—which, for no good reason, I had been reserving for last. At the empty grave site, in an almost spooky stroke of timing, I located a slim, sinewy man with suntanned skin and hollow bones. A plastic tag on the breast pocket of his uniform identified him by name—none other than Mr. Hollow Bones.

A great deal more congenial than the magistrate's assistant, he was also more informative. I learned that, not only was he on duty the night the body was removed, but twenty-four hours prior to that, had been present when it came onto the premises. "I was suspicious," he told me, "when the supervisor called me away from my coffee break. We are entitled to two fifteen minutes breaks per shift—union rules. I had gone only five minutes into my first when they sent me to do an urgent job. In my line of work, that's odd. Who ever heard of an emergency burial?"

Hollow Bones scratched his head.

"I hurried to get my shovel," he explained, "and by that time, the drivers of a van had already got the body loaded onto the cart, having brought it from the morgue."

Mysterious conditions, indeed.

"He'd been a large man, I'd say, guessing by the weight and size of the sack," Hollow Bones continued. "I buried it quickly, just like they told me. I didn't bother to ask questions. Why would I? In this work, a body is just another body. My job is to return it to the earth."

He admitted doing so hastily.

"Under the circumstances," he confessed, "I suppose I didn't dig as deep a hole as I normally would have—the night being dark, and all."

I thanked Hollow Bones and left him to the eternal work of restoring bodies to the earth.

NOT ABOUT THE LAND

I passed the outskirts of the cemetery just before dusk. Taking a glance over my shoulder, I glimpsed the sun as an orange globe touching its base to the peaks of the hillsides. Their jagged forms, outlined in strokes of black, had the bold illusion of a painting—yet never had felt so real. Below them, the cemetery spread over the field, its cement and granite markers rising from parched ground like rows of broken teeth. In an unearthly sort of way, it was one of the prettiest views I've ever seen in Hero.

Winding my way back to the Old City, I came to the arching gateway where I paused to rest at my favorite rock. Purchasing coffee from the roving vendor, I devoted a few minutes to get my bearings (essentially, to take a periodic reading from some kind of built-in compass). First off, I had yet to overcome the sense of time warp. After lengthy absence, I felt like a perfect stranger to this place. Yet, here was I, once again skimming the dusty, lunar contours of the tiny nation they call Hero. I could have been on Planet Hero, for all I knew.

And what had been the purpose of returning? Officially, it was to analyze, at least stand witness to, the recent public disorder. But the more times I quoted this reason, the more it was beginning to sound like an alibi. Disorder is the generic business of newsmen; I can find it at any location in the world, under conditions of better weather, and where there are beaches in addition to the sand dunes. So, why come to Hero? In addition to the generic disorder, I was beginning to think that the reasons were deeper and more disturbing, if unnameable. Once again, I'd come back to cover a war; specifically, Hero's war. But having been away from it for so long had armed me with a new perspective. Here it comes. I realized, and only upon returning, that Hero is a place where wars are fought with stones.

Wait a minute, though. Time to rethink this. Wars are typically fought over resources; they are fought over control of the land. Stones do not win land (not in modern times as we know it). Okay, so "war of stones" was a slight exaggeration, maybe just the poet in me getting carried away. And maybe, in the end, the stones of Hero may be little more than an image with a lethal idea behind it. Call it poetry, then. Or call it an idea. Call it an inconsistency in the truth, if you have to. Just so long as you don't call it a lie. Just remember that, so far as ideas go, it is easy to get lost in the image. I know I'm not the only one. There are many street poets these days. Of course, if you believe that, you've already fallen for another small lie, another inconsistency in the image. Look again, and see how easy it is to be duped. That's because, in actuality, you won't find many poets in the street. Where you will find them is in the prisons. That's exactly where I went the following afternoon—after having spent the morning covering a grizzly, albeit routine, assignment. I figured the least I could do was bring Hektor the news.

"There has been another militant bombing of civilians," I reported, just in case he hadn't had access to the morning edition of The Chronicle, The Cosmos, or any other of the daily papers.

"I heard," he replied, reminding me that the grapevine of the prison was more efficient than any professional journal.

"It's retaliation, the usual business, except that this time, one of the men wounded was a fighter—like you." Unnecessarily, I pointed out, "Now he has been hurt by his own side."

"I believe where you come from, they call that 'friendly fire,'" he rebutted.

"To me, it feels like self-destruction."

That made him a little defensive.

"We're a passionate people," he rebounded. "In Hero, we say 'fierce in our ideals.'"

"That much, the world has seen," I attested.

"Then, understand something. At the moment, we have this struggle; we accept what suffering it brings. But to accept passively the abuses of our enemies is...*impossible*."

In idea, in image, I recognized the echo.

Closing my eyes, I could even picture the stones.

CHAPTER FIVE

NEIGHBORHOODS

TOUR

WEST SIDE, Hero — By the weekend, even from the modest window of my hotel room, the world was looking a few shades better. After finally managing to get a good night's sleep, I had awaken without the siren of the alarm clock, but instead, to the mildly startling conversations of the birds. The first thing I did was splash cool water on my face from a basin that had been left for me by the room keeper. Then, with cool water dripping down, I promptly decided that the best part of being off-duty was the option of electing not to shave. Admittedly, I looked a little on the rough side, and might easily have passed for one of the locals—if only I'd been able to master The Walk.

In Hero, a good swagger is the best defense (if it isn't an outright defiance; in this case, of its own doom). It's also a place where the only ideal left standing at the end of the day is a blind sided and crippled form of courage—a condition that too often degrades into whiplash. Combining vanity with self-destruction, Hero has made itself a cult—where suffering is the norm, redemption a fugitive concept (not always benign), and fatalism runs amuck. In a casual way, despair has become the habit. Then there are the pleasantries I'm only now beginning to discover. For example, ask a Heroaen how things are going, and he is likely to reply, "not terrible." This is intended as the sincerest form of reassurance. The reasons for coming to such a place continue to elude me, unless, as the locals have repeatedly suggested, "The whole point of coming to Hero is to get out." Maybe so, but it only makes me wonder more what it would feel like to be Heroaen for a day.

In reality, I was born to the sterile affluence of the suburbs—in a technologically advanced country oceans of distance from here. Still, I had known, all my life, that I was destined to leave there. It was the cycle of returning that I had not anticipated. Life has taught me, however, that with every attempt to go home again (to the affluent suburb), I am invariably confronted with a fresh yearning to flee. Irredeemably, I am drawn to environments that are festering and seedy—and teeming with life. These are the places I find interesting. Too bad that coming back to Hero did nothing but revive the ache of old uncertainties, familiar letdowns. I was stricken with the sense that the fullest realities of the city lay just beyond my reach. They were the eyes staring out from the barricade of a mask, in a face that, to this day, remains withheld.

I am the worst kind of loner, I'm told. Still, if anything has the power to save me, it's the sporadic, built-in desire to break out of isolation and seek, for a change, the help of another person. This time, I required someone capable of exposing the underbelly of the city; of providing an unflinching tour of its stark, unapologetic streets. Insensibly, I decided to ask Sophi—delicate, impeccable Sophi, whom, in wildest dreams, I could not picture in an environment other than nice. Wandering back to the Old City, I found her gazing pensively from the balcony of her relic stone building. Then I explained, somewhat awkwardly, what I had in mind. "You're a funny man," she observed, "to be looking for the invisible, or the impossible, or what might be not even there."

Then she smiled with a complicity that caught me by surprise.

"But if it's seedy you want," she declared, "all you have to do is say so."

I did—with the words, "Where can we start?"

Well, there are places in Hero you would never see as a tourist. You are not likely to experience them as a journalist, for that matter, unless something newsworthy, like a shooting, has occurred there. In spite of that, or maybe because of it, these are predominantly the places where real lives are lived, out of sight and out of reach to most outsiders. This is because Hero, for all its notoriety, is an intimate city—newly introduced to me by way of the gymnasium, the book store, and the police station next door to the bordello. I was impressed. Like all disparate elements that manage to fit, they dotted the narrow passages with a quaint, almost bland, precision—proof that city planning can be no more random than the universe. It attests not only to the design of the ancient architects, but to their genius, with the end result that Hero is the labyrinth to beat all labyrinths. And so far, we have not got past the street where Sophi lives.

Our tour began at Rix, the full service, Open-24-Hour coffee shop capable of filling in as a closet—having appropriate dimensions for the job. But where Rix had been denied its fair share of space, it had been more than compensated by its location. Occupying the northeast corner of the Old City's central plaza, it offered a sweeping, unimpeded view of The Square. The most notable feature there would be the obelisk— Hero's most venerated structure. The people here say the slate tower was not built, but had sprung straight up from the primordial sands like a petrified tree. And, while its date of origin has yet to be calculated by science, local lore maintains that the obelisk featured on Heroaen ground long before the passage of men's footsteps. No doubt the first Heroaens attributed a mystic significance to the tower, for they set if off with a large area where no additional structures were built— a zoning law that persists to this day. The city square, then, is defined by this swatch of empty, open space. At the frame, however, the physicality drastically changes. On all four sides, The Square's cobbled streets are lined with shops, diners, and makeshift outdoor stalls offering all manner of products and diversions.

Inside Rix, where weekend crowds mean standing capacity only, we fueled up on coffee and fried sweet bread beside the counter. If I was at all self-conscious about fitting into the local scene, it took but one sip of the piping hot liquid to betray me completely. I remarked that my drink had the consistency of motor oil.

"Naturally," Sophi acknowledged. "In Hero, this is how we like it."

"Good stuff," I choked, faintly and with a grimace. I swallowed the rest of the bread without chewing—in an irrational attempt to prevent the coffee from burning out my insides. I realized that, of the many strong coffees I'd imbibed in Hero, I had yet to experience, by local definition, the real thing.

Facing no small challenge, we began jostling our way from the counter toward the exit. In spite of my being a good foot taller than Sophi, it was she who proved the more assertive of the two of us. I am convinced this marks the authenticity of a native. Cheerfully, she asked, "Shall I show you the Hero of my childhood?" To address me, she was obliged to glance not only backwards, but upwards. It was the first time I realized how exquisitely compact she was. A virtual powerhouse.

"By all means," I agreed, reaching over her head to push open the door, "let's go."

WE BEGAN by braving the humanity that had swarmed into the streets (a regular weekend occurrence). Elbowing through the crowd, we pressed our way through passages impossibly carved into the rocky hillside. Finally reaching the apex, we confronted what appeared to be a nondescript warehouse. This was the gym. At ground level, it was fitted with the kind of corrugated metal door that is pulled down like a window shade and secured with a padlock. Producing a key from her pocket, Sophi deftly unlocked it.

"I know the owner of the building," she explained. "To help out, I look in on the place—sort of as a favor." Leading me up the unlit stairwell, she cautioned, "Step carefully. Some of the boards are loose."

Reaching the second level, we entered a room strewn with little more than a few mats held together with strips of duct tape, crisscrossed in spots but in no particular pattern.

"It has always looked like this," she explained. "Barely anything here. When I was a girl, it was used for different functions. By day, it was a kindergarten. In the afternoon, it was turned over to the older boys, who used it to practice their sport."

"Boys' sport" in Hero is an oblique reference to the art of hand-to-hand combat, practiced in a variety of forms that, while encompassing distinctive styles and philosophies, can be distilled to a single discipline. In a word, it looks very much like boxing. Evidence of it was suggested by the assorted apparatus on the far side of the room. A stuffed cylindrical bag, as bulky as a person, hung from the ceiling by a heavy chain. Elsewhere, a speed bag, the size of a human head and the shape of a cocktail olive, dangled in midair at approximately eye level. On the floor lay a padded pair of gloves.

Perusing the room, Sophi's expression grew wistful.

"It doesn't look like much," she said, "but I spent many hours here when I was a child in kindergarten; and when I was older, as a school girl." Coyly, she added. "Sometimes, when there were contests, my friends and I came up to watch the boys."

I replied, "Why doesn't that surprise me?"

Sophi blushed, but in the next moment grew serious.

"Sport is important to us in Hero," she stated, adding proudly, "These days, even girls can try things."

In spite of the deep-rooted resistance to social reform (and to change in general), there has been a recent consensus toward expanding educational opportunities for women. Included in the agenda is a new emphasis on women's sport and physical fitness. Developments in this area are generally regarded by Heroaens as positive change.

"As for the building," Sophi sighed, "the man who runs it is out of town. We don't know yet what will happen." For the time being, the gym appeared abandoned. Like a lot of things in Hero, its future must be added to the long list of other uncertainties.

Back in the street, we progressed at a snail-like pace, hindered by my relentless need to poke nose into storefront after storefront. Within a block, the exploration yielded an apothecary shop which, in both appearance and odor, surpassed my prior notions of authentic medieval. Jars of identified (though unrecognizable) substance crowded the shelves from wall-to-wall. Of these, "Poisons" was easily the most eye-catching (its popularity encouraged, if indeed indicated, by the prominence of the sign). Just as intriguing was the group of jars beneath it, promising "Antidotes." While the man at the counter patiently educated me on both categories, Sophi, having more pragmatic objectives, drifted to the section devoted to matters of laundry. Instead of being sold the perfect chemical bleach, she was simply advised, "If you really want to whiten something, leave it out in the sun." The moral of the lesson was then granted us both. "Every poison contains its own antidote; every stain the chemical secret to rinse itself clean." In Hero, such purifying magic is even evident in the weather. "You can see it on a clear day," our apothecary proclaimed. "The sun bakes the stones to ash."

MOON

"There is a part of Hero I neglected to show you," Sophi announced. In spite of the casualness of her voice, something told me the oversight was deliberate. Perhaps it was the way she added, "It is the *largest* part."

She meant it in both the literal and figurative sense. The "largest part" of Hero turned out to be the sprawling deserts where no Heroaens are known to live. "Most of our land is uninhabitable," she explained, "just the way we like it." As with the finer points of language, or the motor oil coffee, this is another aspect of native life I expect never to entirely grasp. Then again, staring out at the empty expanses, I may have a chance at coming close. To arrive at them, we took detours over abandoned half roads, partially constructed highways, and a full assortment of false impasses. Along the way, we slipped unnoticed passed military checkpoints—and with alarming ease.

"When you're a native," Sophi explained, "you learn to go around."

This was something of a revelation to a foreigner like me. With chagrin, I dredged up the ill memory of long delays at the myriad checkpoints dividing all sides of the city from its surrounding suburbs which, in turn, are subdivided from each other and, ultimately, from the interspersed stretches of land. On a map, the checkpoints appear to form the partitions of a beehive. But, as I learned from Sophi, where the army erected its dividing walls, the natives had cut trap doors.

Within a mile of the last checkpoint, we passed a decrepit farmhouse in the middle of a field—the nearby acres burnt and littered with splotches of black. "This used to be an olive grove," Sophi explained, "thick with the fattest of trees—or so they tell me. Since I was a little girl, though, all I ever saw were the stumps. I asked my father, 'Is this Hero, or is it the surface of the moon?'"

It was evidence, of course, that the Imperial Army had paid a visit. An unofficial scorched earth policy had been in effect for nearly a decade, justified by the state as a defense against rebels who might rely on such outposts as safe houses.

"An old farmer lives here with his donkey," Sophi continued. "His wife and children fled to the city a long time ago, but he won't leave the land. Says his people have been working these fields since the very beginning, and he's going to stay so long as there is a place in the world called Hero."

There's a place in the world called Hero, alright.

And parts of it look like the surface of the moon.

SMOKE AND GUNS

Mondays are greeted in the press room with a fanatic, if narcissistic, ritual. At 7 AM, we gather around Pea Nuts' desk to pilfer his coffee while singing the praises of our profession. Eagerly, we are treated to a pep talk from our Editor-in-Chief, delivered from over the top of the bookcase that doubles as his podium. This week, it began with a particularly useful proclamation. "Writing, my friends, is a mental illness," Pea Nuts chirped, "a specialized compulsive disorder." When few of us bothered to disagree, the session broke up. In the staff kitchen, refilling our coffees, my colleague Zoey insisted on re-addressing the topic with her doleful concession, "Maybe what we do really is a mental illness."

I said, "Well, it's not a hobby."

"But let's admit, Teheda, it has its perks—especially for you." She added mopefully, "At least you get to chase corpses all day."

She, on the other hand, is obliged to spend hers rummaging the city for "oddities worth noting."

Zoey, a native Heroaen and local reporter, joined The Chronicle two years ago to cover Lifestyles (added to the lineup as part of the bureau's efforts to expand coverage to special interests; and to acknowledge that, as Zoey puts it, "there's more to Hero than smoke and guns"). Her desk is one file cabinet over from mine, making Zoey my closest colleague (by location, though by no means, affection). Candidly, she regards me with a contempt she considers "justifiable"—even if I'm not supposed to take it personally. That's because, while submitting to the lesser title of "Staff Writer," she ever aspires to the loftier status of "Bureau Chief" (my job). For that matter, as she likes to bring up, she is still awaiting the melamine name-and-title plaque to affix to the front of her desk (an item I was issued on my first day back; she's right, the inequities abound). "Don't worry, you'll get your promotion," I reassured her. "And when you do, you can have my Bureau Chief plaque—so long as you remember to blot out the name." At the time, Zoey turned over my offer with great thought. "Fine," she replied. "But what about the 'bureau' part?" Gradually catching onto the subtlety of Zoey's humor, I now understand that the "bureau" she refers to is the physical one—in a word, my desk. She claims it is larger than her own.

From the staff kitchen, getting back to our desks involved the long march down the corridor—another ritual of Monday mornings. Stoically, we embarked on the path cradling our coffees. Along the way, I couldn't help but detect Zoey's gaze— analyzing me—from behind a set of dark, horn-rimmed glasses resting midway down the slope of her nose.

"How many cups are you averaging, Teheda?"

"Since I've been here? About seven."

"Hero will do that to you. It will give you an addiction."

"What is it about you people? You can't seem to be happy without one—an addiction, I mean."

"Of course, we like our addictions," she asserted. "They keep us alive."

"Yeah, but it's not just the coffee. It's everything about this place. The coffee, the stones, the violence. It's all so obsessive. I've never known a Heroaen to do anything half way. Take these riots, for example. Every few years, a new eruption. Just like clockwork. I've never met people so in love with the futility of their obsessions."

"Someone has to give you war jocks something to write about."

"That reminds me, I'm working on a story. The title will be, 'Hero's War of Stones,'—and its hero is none other than the late Commander."

Zoey stiffened. Apparently, my irreverence had hit a chord. I guess some topics are too tough to bring up—even in a newsroom. The dead Commander was one of them.

"What would you have us do, Teheda? Sit back idly while they pick us off, one by one? May hell freeze over before that happens. In Hero, you can count on this much—until every last Heroaen is dead and buried, we'll keep raising our children to be brave."

"You're right, Zoey. There must be something in the water."

"What can I say?" she quipped. "We're only here for the world to make fun of. You think we're crazy, or old-fashioned, or backwards."

"All of the above," I affirmed, "but not worse than the rest of us. But I do think that if everyone were a martyr, the human race would shut down. And where would that leave Hero?"

It was a baffling question to us both, and from which we retreated to the respective territories of our desks. For Zoey, that encompassed the memos, photos, and news clippings amassing there as if powered by an independent will. They were testimony to a city rife with "notable oddities." Staring at the piles, I thought about convincing Zoey that the abundance of her material could make covering Lifestyles easier than covering the war; then maybe she would not resent my plaque and desk so much. Instead, I looked on lazily as Zoey rifled through her stacks.

Mine was the same assignment as always—come up with something surprising to say about Hero, its conflicts, and its torments; and while my beat was the war, the more shocking a statement, the better. In last Thursday's magazine edition, I apparently succeeded a little, although I'm still not really sure why. In the wake of the ransacking of the morgue, I had written an opinion piece suggesting that "Hero, on a good day, is a temporary shelter for humanity's condemned." Personally, I had liked the image. Luckily, so had Pea Nuts—less for aesthetic reasons than for the fact that it provoked an influx of heated letters to the editor. Ranging from dismal agreement to livid outrage, the readers' responses provided just the kind of controversy that he, as Chief Editor, loves. Poking head out from the barricade of mail in his office, Pea Nuts had beamed, "It's beautiful, Teheda! You're onto something."

"Yeah," I agreed, "a tornado."

But I smiled to think how, since my nonsense ("load of crap") story on the beggar girl, I'd managed to convince Pea Nuts there was still hope for me; that, with enough grimness, I would yet manage to salvage my writing career. I owed a great deal of the turnaround to my subsequent article about viewing the Commander's corpse. Weirdly enough, the newly missing status of the corpse only made me vulnerable to allegations that I'd made the whole thing up; as in, never got into the morgue, lied about seeing the body, etc. (A rival newspaper even published a headline titled, "Sure, What Corpse?")

Still, I was puzzled over the attention my latest "Temporary Shelter" piece had, in effect, stirred up. Focusing on the mob's recent ransacking of the morgue, my article's only shock value had been an unsparing look at what I called Hero's "festering resentments"—a grievous list aimed at the ruling government, its passive international observers; and at Heroaens themselves. But I didn't think I was saying anything new. I had simply forgotten that, in the universe of Pea Nuts, "festering resentments are what make people fun."

IN THE DIRT

In a tiny nation choked for land, an astonishing amount of it is raked over to the dead. At the cemetery on my third visit, it took even longer to find the way. On the trail I had come to memorize, each step sunk me deeper into fissures; each advancement kicked up increasing clots of dirt. I walked on ground that felt as if, at any minute, it might start buckling. And, as on the first occasion, I passed the hundreds of crooked, sun-bleached headstones placed there for naming the dead. The difference was that, on this day, I saw them more—and saw them with a new importance—as objects can become important when one of their number goes missing. Gradually, I arrived at the plot that was lacking the headstone, or rather, the one it never had. Moreover, it was bereft of its contents. From the edge, it looked like a gigantic buzzard had swooped down and taken a gouge.

In reality, of course, the case seemed to assume the classic shape of a missing person—a dead one. But this raised problems. Primarily, *it's just not that easy to go missing in Hero.* On a staggering level, human existence here—if not its activity—is accounted for down to the numbers. It is measured with incalculable control. This renders, at times, a resemblance to the experience of laboratory mice.

Reductively, there are two categories of human specimen in Hero: natives and foreigners. Better yet, as Zoey has suggested, "Just think of Heroaens as the local fruit; foreigners the outer peel—wrinkly." With few exceptions, Wrinkly Peels fall into two categories: professionals and tourists. Presumably, professionals are here for a specified purpose, are required to announce it on paper and, accordingly, must be registered with their employer, their country's embassy, and the Heroaen Central Governing Board (CGB). Tourists, when they choose to come here, must register with the Central Visitor's Bureau (CVB). On average, Hero hosts about three tourists a year. Fruits are accounted for at birth with the Central Registry, in addition to the aforementioned CGB.

In theory, there is a third (if invisible) category: "Other"— defined universally as the individual belonging to no place and no one. Clearly, though, our missing body dead meant a whole lot to somebody living. That ruled out "Other."

And yet, it had been seven days since our grounds keeper, Hollow Bones, quietly submitted to CGB the report of a plundered grave plot. Since then, there had been no inquiries— from agency or citizen—and no sign of investigation. The police had filed no records of missing persons. And certainly, no one had gone out of their way to tip off the press. I myself was only aware of the case due to an internal suction device that, like a vacuum cleaner, devours obscure flakes of information (and which Pea Nuts hails as my worthiest talent). In any event, signs seemed to point to an unlikely scenario—that not a single living person had bothered to notice the death.

And yet, we are talking about a society where every citizen who dies will have some connection with the living—regardless of how that relationship may have gone. The truth about Hero is that people are far more likely to be abandoned in life than in death. This is based, I think, on the unwavering faith that death resolves all conflicts of the living; and, at the very least, one can expect civility—if not equality—in returning to the dust. Moreover, Hero is a clan society, where every family claims an entire village of extended family. In the end, no matter how estranged or indifferent, someone, somewhere, knows where you are. Considering this, the prospect of the forgotten pauper, a nobody's nobody, was not only looking more unlikely. It was beginning to look impossible.

Hero, however, is a place where the impossible regularly occurs.

An exam question once asked me to define the term, "irony." My first solution was to peer at the paper of the girl sitting next to me. In response, she'd covered her paper with her ponytail. I used up the next few minutes dreading the fates that were certain to accompany my flunking out of high school—like flipping hamburgers to infinity, or getting my own private dorm room on skid row. In a sweaty panic, I then managed to scrawl on my paper the definition of irony as "something that is true even though it doesn't make sense." Although the answer had been good enough to get me past high school, I had no idea what irony was, or what it meant, or if it had anything to do with real life. Many years later, it took but a brief stay in Hero to teach me a more exacting definition of "ironic." It is, in Heroaen terms, the phenomenon of logic turned inside out, or set upon its head. It is this very inversion that makes irony so cruel, and yet so funny. In the spirit of irony, then, it was by its own attempt to suppress an uprising that the municipal authority succeeded in igniting one. Its prohibition of the Commander's funeral achieved no less than to further inflame the masses, who, taking matters into their own hands, immediately ransacked the morgue. Coming up short of the Commander's body, they took to rioting and looting the streets. With GU-2 running full force, the clamor of festering resentments was growing louder in decibels by the day. The mob's grievance, moreover, was motivated by a teething revenge. Someone had denied them their martyr, had dared to steal from the living that honor which is owed to the dead.

Compounding matters, a body had now been exhumed—in a real sense, stolen—from an unmarked pauper's grave. Side by side, the two corpses made not only strange bedfellows; they made a pretty hallucinatory pair, like mirror images reflecting a set of opposites. Okay, let's say what I had was not evidence so much as an ache, one that, like the gaping ground, I could not begin to put a name to. And I have tried. The fact remained that Hero was now missing two bodies. If one had been prince, the other pauper, the age-old riddle is which of the twins came first? The other possibility is that they had never been separate.

ETHICS OF RISK

Well, if the connection failed to convince Pea Nuts, at least it would provide him an excuse to subject me to yet another "Pal" ("I'm concerned for you") lecture. I had to consider this as I was weighing the risks. The first was that I'm a war correspondent and not a detective. In an unfortunate manner of speaking, I was in over my head (and considering having just come from the site of an empty grave plot, this image does not strike as entirely happy). More to the point, without a name or body, the Commander remained for me a man without identity. Yet, his death hovered like a storm cloud over the tense, bewildered city. I raised my eyes from the coffee grinds at the bottom of my cup. Above them, a clock on the desk announced that the time was six. At seven, I planned to submit to Pea Nuts my

byline for the upcoming edition. That meant I had exactly one
hour to convince myself it was a risk worth taking.

I also hadn't slept for the past seventy-two, so that by ten
o'clock—three hours later—I was either running on insomnia,
or a virtually empty tank. The sensation was about the same—a
little like burning low-grade fuel in a finely-tuned engine. Every
now and then, some internal aspect of the mechanism goes
clunk. If it wasn't yesterday's insomnia, it might have belonged
to the night before. These are the days when it's easy to lose
track. I have heard that in the absence of sleep, memory is the
next thing to go. That could also explain my lack of recall when
next confronted by Pea Nuts with the question of professional
ethics I supposedly learned once.

"I brought you back to cover the violence, not incite it," Pea
Nuts said gruffly. "Or didn't you learn that in the College of
Journalism, Teheda?"

"College? What college?" I answered. "I barely remember
finishing high school. Anyway, Pea Nuts, I thought you brought
me back to uncover the truth."

"There's truth, and there's responsible journalism," he
replied. "Which are we talking about?"

"If I had the answer," I said, "I'd have been home hours
ago—like a normal person. What am I saying? I don't even
have a home. I forgot, I live in a hotel room. Anyway, I stayed
around in case you had, um, reservations."

"'Reservations,'" he huffed. "You got that right. One hell of
a story you're asking me to publish, Pal. And I won't even ask
where you got your information."

"First duty of a newsman is to protect his sources," I reminded
him. "Professional ethics, remember?"

Code of ethics aside, he knows there's no chance in hell I'd
tell him.

"Okay, so you don't like the piece," I conceded. "And you're
less than confident about my sources. Still, the work is the
work; the least you can do is trust my judgement. And listen,
the hour is late. Or better yet, take a look out the window. See
that? We're still in Hero. Beyond that, I can't tell you a thing.

Pretty soon, I won't know what my own name is. Pea Nuts, just tell me what you've decided to do."

"I'm going to print it," he said.

"Good," I nodded. "I figured as much."

Okay, so that part was pure bravado. The truth was, I hadn't figured on much of anything, but rather had spent the evening in trepidation and dread. None of that seemed to matter, now. Moreover, I finally took a good look at Pea Nuts. It had taken me that long to notice the dark circles under his eyes. Like talking to my own reflection in a mirror, I said, "Pea Nuts, why don't you go home and get some sleep?"

BLOOD HAS A SMELL

In the gym, the air is ripe with sweat and exhalation—the slow combustion of human exertion when lacking an exhaust pipe. It is a reservoir of bodily secretions fitted with its own chemical rules, where to breathe means to suck up all the spent endeavors that have been left over. Here and there, even as the room is empty and long inactive, I catch whiffs of the metallic traces of blood. Some people claim that blood has no smell, but that it leaves an iron deposit on the tongue that, once tasted, is never forgotten. To this day, I cannot be sure where that kind of tasting stops—or where the smelling begins. I can confirm from experience, however, that the high point of all gymnasiums is the staleness—within the stagnation, the permanent mercurial drift of lockers stuffed with unwashed socks. And the spirit of the odor has remained.

My reputation as a drifter is pervasive. Maybe that's why no one takes me seriously when I talk about settling in Hero. Not only do people know me better than I do, they know enough to sense that I am making a joke. After weeks of living in a hotel room, however, I did finally succumb to the nagging idea that I needed to move. Typical of the Old City's rentals for the transient, my new apartment consisted of a spare room in a crumbling building furnished with a single lightbulb, a naked mattress atop an iron bed frame, a cane chair with a fractured leg, a porcelain wash basin on a fold-up poker table, and no desk. I was hardly inclined to complain for several reasons: firstly, because I have occupied rooms of a similar character under a wide variety of conditions, and on an unbelievably large number of continents; secondly, because the rent was negligible. Upon my inquiry about the fee, Sophi had said, "Don't mention it."

I was living in the room across the hall from the gym. It came about as a result of my having disclosed to Sophi my need to be closer to the city; that, increasingly, news was more likely to break in the urban center than in the countryside. For a reporter, the ease of commute is no mere matter of convenience; it is a daily gamble based upon developing events. Noting this aspect of my work, Sophi became inspired with a sudden idea. After breakfast at Rix, she led me back to the humble building that met the street with a corrugated metal door. Clicking open the heavy padlock, she proceeded up the stairs, bypassing the entrance to the gym. Across the narrow, musty hallway, she unlocked and pushed open the door to a side apartment. "I have already told you, it doesn't look like much," she said, then dropped the key into my hand.

I moved in—though not entirely without apprehension. The mysterious circumstances of my occupancy of the apartment continued to haunt me. Moreover, I gleaned scant relief from Sophi's assurance, "I checked it out with the owner. He approves of there being a tenant."

I'd been inhabiting the place for two weeks before my next visit to the prison. Taking the visitor's seat opposite Hektor, I stuffed a parcel through the vertical bars.

"Another gift?" he asked.

"Call it a tribute," I corrected. "There is coffee this time—in addition to the sausage."

Although I was there to speak of other matters, and possessed no reason to connect Hektor to my new residence, I casually remarked that I had moved closer to the city.

"Congratulations," he said blandly. "That is always more convenient."

"The best part is that I don't have to go far to buy the sausage and the coffee," I joked. "That makes visiting you easier."

He smiled the way a man smiles who already knows what you are about to tell him. Better yet, he knows something that you don't. In the time remaining to our allotted visit, he filled in the details.

"Let me get this straight," I retraced. "My landlord is you?"

"What do you think of that?" he returned, in his habit of question-for-question. Wryly, he slipped another cigarette between his teeth.

"I think I owe you some back rent."

He waved away the suggestion with his cigarette hand—not an easy gesture when the wrists of both hands are cuffed together.

"The payment is in the sausage," he replied, "and, of course, the coffee."

LONG WAY HOME

Acquiring the building had been the product of a persistent dream, conceived in private, and nursed in dank quarters long before his hands touched the clanking tune of the keys. Hektor bought it last summer—ten months after leaving the prison where he'd been incarcerated since age sixteen. Although he'd been busted for leading a farm strike (a relatively minor offense), he was destined to serve no less than a twelve-year jail term—an excessive sentence, even by Heroaen standards. "Five times, my application for parole was stamped 'REJECTED.' Each time, I asked, 'how come?' Judge said I'd been 'born under the sign of a troublemaker.'" Hero is notorious for its arbitrary justice, but Hektor's may be the first recorded case of justice by zodiac.

At long last, relief came when a lawyers' group advocated on behalf of prisoners' rights. Along with eleven other fortunates,

Hektor rolled his belongings—a few books and a toothbrush—into his spare shirt. Outside the loading gate, he took a parting glance before packing himself into the back of the wagon painted "prisoner-transport." On board, he was fitted with the mandatory blindfold and driven an indeterminate distance; perhaps, as he suspected, in quarter-mile circles. When the moment came for the soldier to peel off his blindfold, Hektor's eyes squinted in pain. Bracing himself against the sunbeams piercing the center of his pupils, Hektor noted the ditch beside the road. The rickety vehicle, not much different from the one that first delivered him to the gates of the prison, was now creaking to a halt some miles away. It stopped at the bend of a rocky path which bore the closest nearby resemblance to a road. In succession, each prisoner in the wagon stood up for the soldier to cut away his blindfold. Each then took turns growing dazed at the sight of the barren land. "What's the matter?" the soldier taunted. "Expecting paradise?"

"What does it matter?" Hektor replied. "We are free."

Man by man, the released prisoners stumbled out of the wagon, reconnecting the bottoms of their feet to the ground. In the near distance, the spires of ancient stone structures loomed, as untouchable and elusive as the fog. They belonged to the place that, in remote memory, they knew they had once called Hero. And now they knew that, to regain it, all they had to do was walk there. They set out as a pack, dwindled to a cluster, then fell to single file as if by instinct. That became the only sensible way to traverse the narrow, unfamiliar, or overgrown paths. Along the way, the freed men continued to diverge, armed with the recollection that their homes lay in scattered directions. Some dissolved into the sprawling desert where there were no roads; others branched into the avenues that stretched along the suburbs; still others fed into the labyrinthine streets leading toward the center of the city. At length, Hektor all alone arrived at the mouth of the passage that marked his old neighborhood, the familiar complex of buildings, and the yellow doorway. Rapping his knuckles against the wood, he soon stood face-to-face with the woman who, wearing curlers and a faded, floral house dress, appeared much older than he remembered (due to the No Visitors penalty slapped on rioting inmates, he hadn't seen her in over a year). Now, like his own earlier reaction to sunlight, it was as if someone had lifted her blindfold. He said, "Mama, I decided to take the long way home." The next thing he did was ask for a cup of her coffee.

TASTE OF THE SOIL

In the morning, Hektor brushed aside the edges of a curtain in the kitchen.

"Autumn," he remarked, "the season of renewal."

He drew a breath, savoring the rawness it tickled at the back of his tongue.

From the table where she sorted the beans, his mother answered, "It's the taste of soil."

"I think it's more the dust," he corrected gently. "Autumn blows in with the dust storms."

It had been spring when they first told Hektor his freedom was coming. From that season forward, the world-as-he-saw-it transformed. With such power did he again look forward to living that while resting, he felt weightless. Whipped along in a frenzy of lightness, he danced in timing to the exhalation of the doves. With closed eyes, he remembered the family grove with its coffee trees planted row after row. And from the blur of the branches, he counted a thousand white petals among the assembly of dots. Once freed, he crossed the desert to reach the home where he surprised his mother at the doorstep. In that instant he was happy, in spite of the splotches of dirt on his shoes.

He discovered, however, what had become of the family's coffee groves during his absence. The army, paying a visit, had enforced The Authority's scorched earth policy—justified, officials say, as part of the strategy to destroy potential hideouts for rebels. But as rumor maintained, the Central Planning

Division (CPD) harbored its own designs. "They want to build a highway where the coffee grows," Hektor conjectured. Although no construction had yet begun, the family later received marginal compensation for the value of the land as determined by the CPD's assessor. This happened in spite of Hektor's insistence that, "We never agreed to sell it."

NO JOB IN HERO

What he learned next was that there was no work to be had in Hero—illustrated in graphic terms by the recent arrest and interrogation of a neighborhood boy. "He'd been handing out pamphlets," Hektor reported, which had turned out to be harmless—mere advertisements for the laundry service he was attempting to launch. The boy's arrest was yet another sign of the government's heightened surveillance of all activities that might be regarded as suspicious. Moreover, it informed Hektor of the scarcity of jobs. In his neighborhood alone, six families had lost the livelihoods of their farmlands. "In Hero, everyone longs for a job," Hektor explained. "And in Hero, no one can stand having a job."

DIRTY SHOES

On paying his mother a visit, I confirmed Hektor's own description of a woman attired in floral house dress and big hair—coiffured neatly into rows of plastic curlers. Over piping hot coffee (offered as soon as I stepped in the door), she told me that her first concern for her jail-freed son had not been his unemployment, but something even more material—and more immediate. "I was appalled at the condition of his shoes," she disclosed. The weariness of their leather filled her with an irrepressible gloom—exacerbated by her son's admission that he'd received them by donation. "He said, 'The Prison Exit Committee is a charity, Mama, not a department store.'"

Hearing Hektor's words passed along from the lips of his mother, I recognized a glimmer of the deadpan humor that had disarmed me when first meeting her son. Matter-of-factly, she added, "As a mother, I was concerned about his prospects."

"For a job?" I asked (thinking I'd missed a loop in the conversation).

"I meant the other kind of prospect," she corrected. When I still drew blank, she posed, "Just think about it. How does a young man with tired shoes supposed to go winning a bride?"

NO DATE

"It was not a 'date,'" Hektor corrected—when I next had occasion to broach the subject. "It was an 'arrangement.' Please understand," he clarified meanly, "we are talking about a girl chosen by my mother with the interference of a neighbor, which assured that her assets would include crooked teeth and acne. If I know my mother, it promised not to be an 'arrangement' so much as a 'setup.'" And then he laughed. "But, of course, I had no idea."

In early evening he approached the door of a third floor apartment nestled in one of the more ancient streets of the city. The door was painted the same ochre color as the linen of his shirt. He reached into one of the neatly pressed pockets to withdraw the slip of paper bearing the young lady's name. Rehearsing, he whispered, "Sophi."

"She opened the door with one hand, and had a bowl of coffee in the other," he recalled. "Then she'd looked at me with this funny expression. Without words, she turned her back and vanished behind the door. I waited. Moments passed. And I wondered, what sort of bad impression have I made?"

"She didn't like you?" I surmised, provoking from him a gentle shrug.

"I think she didn't want to do this."

"Well, what then?"

"I had no choice," he shrugged. "I tried the best I could."

He took her to the winter carnival, an idea to which she assented blankly. "At least there, I thought I could show off at the manly contests." In progressive stages, Hektor proceeded to empty his wallet for the privilege of putting his motor skills to the test. In the process, he was required to toss hoops onto posts too large for them to fit on, and that were planted unreasonable distances away. "The contests are rigged," one of the players informed him. "It's like the lottery." He replied, "Yes, but at some point, the odds must turn. It's like life."

For Hektor, the odds didn't turn quick enough to save his effort, whose sum prize amounted to a fluffy pink dog stitched from polyester and stuffed with cotton batting. He decided to remedy the letdown by suggesting they duck into the nearby pet store, where they spent a few moments admiring real, live creatures. Then, with his final dollar, Hektor purchased the sandwich of spicy peppers and sausage that Sophi didn't care to eat. At eight o'clock, they stopped at the arch of the city and, according to Sophi's suggestion, paused to sit for a moment beneath the canopy of stars. In the brief, blue light, Hektor stole peeks at the crystalline slopes of her face, unsure whether to credit such beauty to winter, or to Sophi. He concluded, at length, that the two were inseparable.

On the long walk to restore Sophi to her doorstep, every street seemed to overtake them in the labyrinth, at the end of which loomed the obligatory, uncomfortable goodbye. It was then that Hektor, standing in the outer space of the open doorway, committed the indiscretion of peering through. "I saw Antigone," he sighed, recalling the vision with a glow. "There she was, balancing on an oversized stool, and in such a curled manner that I could not tell where her knees ended and her elbows began." He also saw—inside that moment—the fulfillment of a promise pre-delivered by the doves.

"In the morning, I said, 'Please choose me.' In the afternoon, she said, 'I will.'" In the evening, Hektor broke the happy news to his mother, who, by next daybreak, had broadcast the announcement of her son's engagement throughout the district. This had the effect of mobilizing, en masse, the women in preparation of festive foods—in quantities vaster than the eyes could see, or the stomach could handle. As described by Hektor, "An orgy of sweets ensued." On the day of the event held in celebration of her engagement, Antigone dressed her bridal doll in a new hand sewn garment and meticulously combed the strands of her hair to a silky sheen. All that was missing were the flowers.

MAYOR OF HERO

Beauty can't possibly be an accident.

I have often thought about that as I watch yet another Heroaen sunrise, or pass a field of red poppies bursting open like flames against a sea of blue. Such sights arm me with great confidence that in the universe, there is an order to things. In reality, though, most flowers do not sprout upon bodies of water, and there is no sea to be seen in Hero. Mixed messages, already—and that's only the beginning. It is still morning.

Hero does not always make sense; and for a fact, it doesn't want to. Instead, the people here grow accustomed to contradiction, and they develop an amazing suppleness in the face of it. I still maintain that I'd come back to record a fuller picture of this bizarre yet potent city—though I don't deny it has been a wayward course. Then again, reality is ultimately subjective, and it depends on where you are standing. If you are the Mayor of Hero, the labyrinth takes on an entirely new set of twists. So far in my coverage, I had yet to pay that man a visit, and it is a blaring oversight. In the overall drama, he is an important, if somewhat distasteful, addition to the cast of players. That is because, in summation, Hero is more than its militants, political prisoners, and elite commandos. It goes beyond its fretting mothers, too; beyond even the ether-reality of its waifs, or the sulkiness of lovers spurned. If Hero were a fairy tale, there are parts of it that are indisputably un-romantic. Pathetic as it sounds, Hero is also the sad-eyed donkey (a whole team of them, I'd say). And beneath the cuteness of that image, it can be downright ugly, because Hero would *not be Hero* if not for the corruption. Maybe Hero is no more than the shards from a pot of broken dreams, or the distress of a revolution that was ripe and has now gone sour. But, for certain, it is one deep cistern of decay.

Within the same month that Hektor was sprung from the prison, the Mayor had been installed into office because of his collaboration with the Empire. Here is how that works. For the scoreboard, Hero has posted two uprisings (though some prefer to call them wars). The Mayor fought the colonizers in the first war (GU-1), and was co-opted by them in the second (GU-2). He is the classic military hero—not necessarily a bad guy, but no model of benevolence, either. A former third place medalist in traditional boxing, his chief contribution in office has been the push to rebuild the sports infrastructure in Hero, offering subsidies to budding athletes and their coaches. So while he had never stood at the top step of the victory podium, in the arena of public relations he is nevertheless touted as the champion of the ring, as well as the champion of the underdog. But here comes the kind of irony I love. Since being co-opted by the Empire in GU-2, he has become the chief suppressor of rebels (though he once was one). And, if one is to believe the word in the street, he is the key proponent in the recent slew of assassinations, endorsed by the state and carried out by its local henchmen. In a word, any citizen marked "rebel" has become an open target. Many Heroaens simply assume the Mayor's involvement in the recent killing of the Commander.

I met the Mayor in The Square. As we began walking west on Canary Boulevard, he pointed out varying signs of progress in a city still battling the spectre of GU-1. "Hero will be revitalized," he beamed. Proof of his declaration could be seen in the strips of remodeled storefronts and the construction of concrete apartments that will be billed as luxury units. I could not deny the impression that Hero, or parts of it, were preparing to be upwardly mobile. But which parts, and for the benefit of whom?

"The boulevard looks great," I reassured him. "And yet, you have your critics. In the street, there is grumbling as to who will be cut out of the picture."

"They are malcontents," he obliged. "In Hero we will always have them. But for our nation to go forward, they must be dealt with."

"Clearly, there has been a lot of 'dealing' going on."

"If you're referring to the elimination of the rebel, well, that was tragic. Understand, of course, that this is Hero. The wars have eaten half of our young men."

"In the past, you fought against the foreign oppression. Yet today, people associate you with it."

"The wars of Hero are funny," the Mayor shrugged. "The tide turns, and the friend of today has a fifty percent chance of becoming the foe of tomorrow. Young men do not understand this. They expect that the world is loyal, which makes them cling to hard ideals. Reality is different. A man who lives long enough will learn that." He seemed okay with the contradiction. "Wars are lonely ventures," he said.

NOSTALGIA

"Because she was young, we gave in to the wish of Antigone's parents to delay our marriage. 'Wait another two years,' they told us. 'What can happen in another two years?'" Hektor's question sounded as rhetorical as the answer was self-mocking: "Only the unraveling of a dream." He added this thoughtful analysis: "Never put off a good dream. It's like buying a bag of coffee. Somewhere on the label—usually the bottom—it is stamped with the expiration date you won't notice until you've taken it home." The date for the wedding itself was derived only after a period of extended negotiation—"like the peace talks."

During the wait, arriving at a normal life was also taking longer than expected. After a time, however, Hektor felt Heroaen again—and actually liked it. This represented progress, for, during the early days home, he'd had a strange longing to be back at the prison. "Inside there, I didn't have to make decisions," he said, "and there was a set routine. We did nothing." In the world again, uncertainty attached itself to his new freedom "like a rash."

He found odd work making deliveries for the grocer, performed repairs around his mother's house, and frequently strolled to Antigone's home to help her with her homework. "Sometimes, I would walk to Old Hero, visit some of the prettier streets," he recalled. "Though naturally, I avoided temptations." (When I delved, he declined to run down the list.) But despite the constructive diversions, Hektor grew bored. Eventually, the condition succumbed to a partial nostalgia.

He sought to remember on paper exactly what had been good about the prison, and his first discovery was that the memory was no longer fresh. Although a mere span of months had passed, the era seemed so remote to him that it may as well have been a life time. Dredging the recesses of a past he thought long buried, he wrote "food" as the first item on the list. Within seconds, the word called up the odor of stale beans and mold-encrusted bread. He crossed off "food" and scribbled beneath it, "coffee." He struck that item immediately, as he remembered there had been none. Continuing, he wrote, "ceiling." In spite of the hours he'd spent staring at it, all he could recall was that the ceiling had been more or less white. The stains, cracks and chips that once interested him could no longer be accessed, had faded to oblivion... "Books," he, thought, jotting down titles with the same obsessiveness that in prison had earned him the nickname, "Scholar." But he realized that, since freedom, he had already reread them all. That left bodily exercise—in its purest form, a mindless act of the will. "I dreamed I was the tiger," he said, "throwing my body against the sides of the cage. I had this unspeakable power. And yet, it is a blind, wild thing. You can't buy it, and you can't soothe it. It does what it wants to do."

HEKTOR'S GYM

I decided my next dispatch from the field would focus on the competing faces of Hero—the burgeoning sites of construction, scattered signs of economic revival, and the promise of jobs—all marred by the recent surge in violence. So, having gathered the Mayor's opinion, I decided it was time to take up the subject up with Hektor. In analysis, we attempted to retrace the roots of the war to Great Uprising 1, proceeding from there to GU-2. Since he had lived at least part of them, and I had recorded at least part of them, we fancied that we were qualified authorities, somehow. After recounting the sacrifices of both conflicts, we tried to name the key achievements. Coming up with scant number, we invariably gave up. Mostly, though, we reflected on the wars' lost opportunities—the kind so easy to identify in hindsight. "Maybe winning a war really is easier than winning a peace," Hektor considered. "Naturally, being Heroaens, we mean to put off victory indefinitely."

But he had his own way of dealing with Hero's contradictions. "If you really try to understand the experience of living," he supposed, "it would frighten you to death." Being Heroaen, however, Hektor was not a man easily frightened, or easily derailed by contradictions he could do nothing about. Thus, when the Mayor announced the offer of subsidies for the revival of athletic ventures, Hektor was the first from his neighborhood to apply. Armed with a tax-exempt grant and a hammer, he purchased a crumbling structure whose appearance on the state's list of condemned properties posed an initial, if temporary, obstacle. He simply understood that part of his grant would be put toward having it removed from the list—with no questions asked. After securing, in similar fashion, the necessary permits, he proceeded to rebuild his dream business from the ground floor up. On completion (a relative term), he posted a hand painted banner over the door to announce it, "Hektor's Gym—The School for Heroaen Boxing." Below the sign, he taped a schedule of the services offered—including aerobic conditioning; power fitness classes; dietary management; self defense technique; disciplined instruction of children; and customized personal training.

During the first week, he received no customers. Resolving to do more to get the word out, Hektor recruited Antigone to draw up a more visually appealing poster. In the resulting graphic, two splendidly endowed boxers faced off in martial contest—if not mortal combat. And their muscles were life-like. Beneath the picture, Sophi contributed the neatness of her hand-lettering while Hektor dictated what she should write. The project completed, the trio stepped back and admired it with self-congratulatory awe. They had made one fantastic poster. Armed with one hundred photocopies of the original, Hektor struck out alone to paste them on strategic walls throughout the streets of the city.

He did not get far. Police arrested him for posting propaganda. Although the charge was bogus, he was detained eight hours before anyone in the Precinct Office would examine his case. He showed the precinct chief the poster. "There has been a misunderstanding," he insisted. "I am a man of business." The policeman, a former wrestler, made an embarrassed apology and released him.

Under the circumstances, Hektor counted himself lucky. He had not been condemned to sleep the full night in the jail cell and, moreover, had narrowly escaped being slapped with a fine. (The Precinct Offices typically charge detainees a violation to cover the cost of processing their paperwork—even in cases where the detention was baseless.) Fortune notwithstanding, Hektor could not help but feel annoyed. Before attracting even a single customer, his new business had hit an unforeseen administrative snag.

That feeling was remedied when, over the next weeks, prospective students began drifting into Hektor's Gym. Most arrived equipped with ample motivation, poor coordination, and little, if any, athletic skill. He devoted the initial month to teaching fundamentals, dissuading the more daring (or delusional) pupils from advancing to activities that exceeded their preparation. They couldn't wait to step into the ring and begin to slam each other. "Boxing is about discipline," he cautioned them. "Until you've mastered the basics, you're not ready to be a fighter. Step in the ring now, you'll get your teeth kicked in." That dampened their ardor. Unrelenting, Coach Hektor exhorted his athletes to work harder at the physical aspects of their training. "Fighting is an art form," he reminded. "Above all, it's about respect." What's more, he acknowledged that the most important thing the sport had taught him was patience and, with that, he grew confident that, over time, the lessons he instilled in his pupils would show fruition. For the time being, however, Hektor continued to long for that elusive prize that all men of his calling long for. He dreamed of the day when Hektor's Gym would produce a champion.

CONTENDERS

Hero is famous for producing contenders. But, like the wars it seems perpetually on the verge of winning, the sport of boxing has never graced this city with a champion. To a number of its graduates, though, the prison's boxing program was no doubt its highest legacy. Of the young Commander, Hektor recalled "He was slow and, with droopy eyes, had the habit of gazing at nothing. You would think he wasn't paying attention, then wham! If you examined his eyes, you saw the slumbering house dog, not the panther." But he recalled (with a rub to his ear), "Of course, the panther was always there. Of us two, he was the younger. And yet, he taught me, this is what a good strike should be."

I could not decide if the excitement in Hektor's voice was pride, envy, or the confounding combination of both. I began to wonder, too, about the many Heroaen males who must come of age within the walls of the prison, and in such close quarters with one another. Prison must approximate, in this sense, one gargantuan family of uncles and brothers. Very likely, Hektor and the Commander would have shared such a bond—with all the loyalty and rivalry it implies. "Years later, he came to my gym like a stranger, and in a shy way. You couldn't see his face inside the headgear. But then he moved, and a recognition—big as light—hit me all at once. Panther was home."

Men long for honor in the places they least can find it. At the gym, they carved a pocket where it was possible to shut out the war. "In there, what matters is the contest," Hektor explained. "Boxing is all about grace—of heart, of mind, of body. In the fight, we give our best effort, and afterwards, embrace. We forgive."

CHAPTER SIX

PERILS

SPEED BAG

HILL SIDE, Hero — I would describe, with great accuracy, how they set upon me. The problem is, I never saw the thugs approach. I'm embarrassed to admit this, if only because I once took pride in the range of my peripheral vision. I had developed it the hard way, from too many fists slamming into the sides of my head. What surprised me more than the assault, however, was my own reaction. Like the sudden appearance of my assailants, the ability to swing my fists took on a spontaneous life. I didn't actually control it, but responded from the naked urgency to live.

It's nice when lost skills revisit, as if they were a service that works on call and charges on a pro-rated basis. Instantaneously, they enabled me to strike out in a flurry—upper cut, right jab, left hook to the temple. I even got out a few kicks, though hardly pretty. Even so, the movements were ferocious in speed and sublimely creative (under the circumstances). Most importantly, they made contact—something my knuckles confirmed.

The targets were a combination of flesh, bone, and the cactus-itch growth of new beards. I counted three aggressors in total: one jacketed in blue, two in khaki, all of medium build, and ranging in age from early twenties to middle thirties. They had at least the appearance of local boys. Had they done more than grunt, I might have been able to tell something by what they uttered. But, because all I could make out were echoes of "Ack!" and "Aggh!"—like in the comics—I was forced to rely on visuals alone. It's strange to think how, by profession, I'm a sort of trained eyewitness. Yet, all I could remember was that.

The event might have lasted less than a minute, making it the quickest round I ever fought—with or without the gloves on. Like the hot breath of a storm, my attackers fled, piling into the back of a jalopy that sped away. I am guessing, by my paranoid sense of such encounters, that the trio may have meant to put me in the car. To their chagrin, the scene did not play out that way. They must have been as stunned by my sudden flash of martial competence as I was. I like to think so, anyway. Moreover, if abduction was their endeavor, they must have decided to abandon the idea in a hurry. For myself, it was not hurry enough. Engulfed in a puff of dust, I watched the car's tail lights shrink and fade back into the stone and mortar landscape.

I decided it was the kind of evening only a goddess, or beautiful guide, could save. Staggering home, I looked for her—the divine face in a slab of broken concrete. I continued to search in patches of fading graffiti, and in the crimped skin of fencing pierced by its own barbed wire. Calling into manholes, I heard the voice echo back through the grate of the drainage ditch; and of course, it was still my own. Nearly home, the only guide I managed to find was the tattered corner signpost—which wasn't very lovely, at that. But a row of street lamps did momentarily flicker on to light my way. With darkness coming fast, dusk could do little but hustle aside. At the corrugated metal door, I clumsily fished for the key among the jingle of coins that, miraculously, had managed to stay in my pocket. With a turn, the padlock yielded with a rasp and a click. Inside, the stairwell was predictably dim, and only after the painful climb did I see the light on. It was not coming from the hallway, as I'd expected, but from the next door gym.

Like an insect, I was attracted to the light. Once inside the gym, I had no choice but to work my loneliness out on the bags. Walking up to the head size leather olive, I began to pommel it. Together, my fists timed precisely to the rebound, and I lost myself in the rapidity of the clank and squeal—to my ears, a primitive form of music. Mesmerized, I don't know how much time passed. All that mattered was that I no longer felt alone.

Eventually, I came to realize that, in fact, I wasn't. Dazed, I finally looked up and saw the figure in the doorway. Leaning against a side of the frame, she had the relaxed posture of someone who'd been standing there for an indefinite amount of time. She said nothing, and I, in turn, had not the soundness of mind to ask Sophi how long she had been watching.

SOPHI'S STREETS

"You look a mess," Sophi remarked, without moving from her position in the door frame.

"Umm, well, something unexpected got added to my day," I replied. "A little scuffle."

While distress flashed across her face, Sophi appeared content to drop the subject. Instead of seeking explanation, she provided one.

"After work, I'd come by to change the lightbulb and do some cleaning—then fell asleep on a corner of the mats. Waking, I saw that it had gotten dark outside."

She indicated the street lights glaring in through the window.

"It's late," I announced. "I should take you home."

Downstairs, we clicked shut the padlock, then began threading our way through the nearly deserted streets. Sophi ignored my limping. Moreover, if she had any nagging curiosity about my condition she managed (almost oddly) to suppress it. I did not share her discipline, instead electing to divulge a question of my own.

"Tell me something," I hedged, searching for tact. "Here we are—*in Hero.*"

I'd placed special emphasis on the word. Sophi nodded, waiting.

"From what I've seen, life is supposed to be old-fashioned. It's no secret that young ladies are supposed to stay at home. Do your parents know where you are?"

With a pout and a sideward glance, she replied, "Not really."

This troubled me. In Hero, the only thing more scandalous than a young woman out alone at night was the prospect of a young woman out wandering *with a man.*

"And yet, you're here with me," I persisted. "Why?"

Sophi flashed her enigmatic smile.

"The secret is Antigone," she confessed.

Falteringly, I made an attempt at comprehension.

"She covers for you?" I asked.

"We cover for *each other*," Sophi corrected. "Of course, we do this in order to get away with things—because it's fun. But mostly, we help each other because we are sisters."

The explanation not only satisfied me, but served as my first glimpse of the stealthy potential of that pair.

In silence, we continued walking. While infernally hot during day hours, Hero's temperatures can drop drastically after nightfall. So, winding through the labyrinth of stark and narrow streets, we began to shiver a little from the cold.

"Look around us," Sophi whispered in the quiet darkness. "It is here that I like to wander; because for me, this is Hero. And remember when I took you to see the desert? For Antigone, that is Hero." She thought some more, and stated, "All of it is Hero."

I took a careful look around while Sophi watched me.

"I think you like it here," she noted. "Why?"

I took a minute to put it into words.

"Maybe because it's this place—these streets, the night—that makes you Heroaen, that makes you Sophi. Maybe the streets here are your prison. Maybe they set you free. If you ask me, that's my guess."

"The streets give me freedom," she said. "But if you want to know what makes me Heroaen, it is that I never thought survival would be this hard."

"But you never thought you'd be this tough, either," I told her.

Sophi smiled at that.

"Funny thing is, all I ever wanted in life was my very own house to keep warm and clean. All that remains in this world are details." Then she asked, "What could it be that you want?"

"I think, the details."

CENSORED

I stumbled into Pea Nuts' office the usual way—by tripping over stacks of manuscripts planted in the aisle just in front of the door. It's his personal paper mine field. A few steps clear of it, I collapsed into the chair opposite his desk. With sore head and cheeks overgrown by bristle, I must have had the raw look of a man trapped for a week in a coal mine. Okay, I have never actually been in a coal mine, so how would I know? (I can say that I've seen the pictures.) At minimum, I had the feeling that I had reached an advanced stage of *chronic fatigue*. This is a modern condition that Pea Nuts does not believe in; claims it's been invented for either economic or political reasons, which I haven't figured out (and neither has he). That's funny, considering he has been suffering it longer than I have.

He said, "You don't look well."

I reached over his desk and poured myself a cup of his coffee—a viscous sediment reeking of burnt elements. Its consistency reminded me of a volcanic eruption, or worse. For a split second, I considered verbalizing what that might be, then lost the thought completely. Instead, I eased myself back into the chair with the agility of a crippled donkey.

"Pea Nuts," I said, "I haven't slept in three days. If you ask me how I'm doing, I'll tell you I'm over the edge. Wrenched out. Barely hanging on. And then, frankly, you'll laugh."

He did—if only to acknowledge the honesty of my statement. Like the best jokes in the world, it's only funny because it's true. I gave Pea Nuts an abbreviated, rather than blow-by-blow, account of my recent street fight—omitting sound effects that hadn't been so informative in the first place. While I decided to spare him the serious details, I thought the part about the fist slamming into my jewels deserved at least a casual mention. Pea Nuts took it all in with the cool composure of a Roman general analyzing the news that half his army has just been slaughtered. Finally, he asked, "What do you think they wanted?"

"Beats me," I replied (and with a poor choice of phrase, I know). I shifted my weight, let out a grimace as the hard edge of a loose joint ground into a nerve. "But it doesn't smell right. I wouldn't be surprised if it was CID trying to send me a message—like a specialized form of hate mail. Apparently, they didn't like some stuff I wrote."

CID—or Central Information Division—is the censorship wing of The Authority. With a reputation for ineptitude, it loosely, sometimes haphazardly, oversees the trafficking of public information. "These are sensitive times," noted Pea Nuts. "All this broo-ha over one dead rebel; in the street, the mobs won't cut slack until they get back a corpse. It's weird—even for Hero. And it's got the CID folks mighty edgy."

It's possible, too, that CID plain didn't like me talking to the Mayor. There was always the chance he'd leak anything he knew for a price—and to the highest bidder (me?). That only strengthened the prospect that I was close to turning over a secret that, according to CID people, should badly stay hidden. Instead of sharing these thoughts with Pea Nuts, I tilted my head back, gulping down the rest of the smoldering potion. My face came up twisted. It just goes to prove that the last sip of coffee is never as good as the first.

DIRTY SECRET

Right next to its corral for the poorest, a section of the sprawling cemetery is set aside for the nation's most venerated tombs. Out of a morose sense of custom, or a melancholy nod to the flaws of history, Sophi concluded our site seeing tour by taking me there. "We call this Hero's Pass, the place our ancestors buried our war dead," she explained, in a voice without emotion. "To this day, we are getting new ones. See the stone sticking up from the dirt over there? He was a boy just seven years old." A few feet from where we stood, a small mound was marked off by a jagged boulder on which was written, in permanent red marker, the child's name, enhanced by a photograph affixed to the stone with pieces of duct tape. Elsewhere, the ground broke into similar rises, designated by crude slabs of granite and overrun by weeds. "Not a fancy place, is it? I think it's a bit of a dump. Then again, you did say you wanted to glimpse the reality of Hero. Does it surprise you?"

"I didn't come to judge things," I maintained. "Just to see, and listen. Most of all, to notice."

"Of course," she relented, "that is your job." And then she smiled, if a little wryly. "I suppose you are now equipped to expose our dirty little secret to the world." With the mildest patience, Sophi watched as I tucked the notebook back into my pocket.

It's one thing to acknowledge the gap between Hero's ideals and its hard reality; and another to accept that, after the clamor of the crowds, the jubilant cries of honor, the fate of the fallen is to end up here. Looking around, I saw a place of decrepitude and sad neglect; but what I understood, and what Sophi was really trying to show me, was the shame.

We left Hero's Pass and began walking, perhaps without intention, in a direction I had been before—toward the pauper's section. If I had any redemptive thoughts left, it was the fledging notion—or faith—that a certain missing body might yet defy its statistical ranking as Hero's First Nobody. With solemnity, I indulged the hope, deep down, that he was not the Forgotten

Man so much as the Unknown Soldier—to whom monuments
have been erected around the world. But as we approached the
plundered grave plot, my heart sank, weighted down by the
solitude of the abyss. It was only then that I saw—or really
paid attention to—the small object protruding from the dirt.
Its location was right about where the headstone should be,
if it hadn't been absent. Moreover, the thing appeared to have
been dropped—or discarded—in a hurry. "It's a shovel," I said.
"Plastic, like the kind that belongs to a child." Casually, Sophi
replied, "It seems so," but with a practiced detachment that
poorly disguised a deeper distress. The presence of the toy must
have struck her as an incongruous, almost grotesque, reminder
of the boy's grave we saw at Hero's Pass—an effect not lost
on me, either. Having previously overlooked the plaything, the
memory of the boy was probably what spurred me to notice it
now.

"Where's the beach?" I asked, in a failed attempt to lighten
the moment.

Raising her eyes from the shovel, Sophi looked stricken.
"I'm not sure what you mean."

"When I see a toy like that, I think of the beach," I explained.
"But your city is encircled by desert."

"You don't need a beach to have sand," she defended. "And
lots of desert children have shovels."

"It was a joke, Sophi."

And I guess a bad one, by the sudden pallor of her face.

"In Hero, the sand is everywhere," she persisted. "Just take
a look around us."

I did, if only to spare her the directness of my gaze while she
knelt, scooped up the child's shovel, and quickly slipped it into
her pocket. "This place saddens me," she said. "A toy has better
places to be than here."

BODY POLITIC

In ancient times, famous thinkers described society in terms of a "body politic." Today, I saw its face appear in the windows of box-shaped tenements. Its legs dangled from the balconies, while assorted limbs clung to the rungs of ladders swinging from the fire escapes. Within minutes, it had swelled onto the rooftops. Finally, it seemed that every square inch of Hero had been smothered by its wrath. Like the crest of a wave, its mouth was beginning to foam, threatening to swallow the tide that would not break—or ease—until the current sucked back the force of its own reflection. It had arrived to demand the return of the dead man; not in miraculous resuscitation, but in the flesh. "We won't settle until we have the hero's corpse back," a citizen told me. "So we are staging a sit-in. Details are in the pamphlet." She handed me one. In addition to a schedule of speeches, it said, "Bring your own lunch." Had the event planners foreseen how their protest march and sit-in would evolve to the sleep-in to top all sleep-ins, they might have added, "Bring your own bed roll."

Making my way toward the obelisk, I passed the morgue before threading under the arch—the unexpected gateway dividing the two sides of the street. From that vantage, the obelisk loomed prominently against the skyline and, on this day, became my compass. I needed one; for, in spite of my increasing exposure to the place, I continued to be lost. I'm sure the disconnection is as much a factor of the mind as the geography, because in Hero, it's possible to look, and look again, without being fully convinced of the planes that one is seeing. Especially on days when the sun is shining, and the light reflective, the city becomes a house of mirrors.

Some distance later, I rounded a sharp bend to arrive at the northeast corner of the plaza. Though pressed for time, I succumbed to the urge to duck into Rix for a paper cup's worth of lavaline coffee. At the counter, I was surprised not to find a line. Beyond it, the chipped marble tables were cleared of their usual crusty plates and crumpled napkins, and aside from the pair of elderly diners slumping over a chess game, the cafe was empty. "A slow day," I remarked to the waitress. "Well, this is Hero," she dismissed, "where politics are the ruin of business. I heard some stores will be closing for the day. The shoppers have all gone to The Square." Asked if she was sorry to be missing the excitement, she replied, "Not at all. All I have to do is look out the window." We both did just that. In addition to the unobstructed view of the obelisk, we could see, in one sweep, the fullness of its shadow, spilling itself across the great urban plain. Beneath the shadow, the legions of ants marching over ground could be discovered, on closer inspection, to be the people.

I walked along the edge of the plaza rather than through it, using the obelisk—or its shadow—as my guide. It was to the left of me, then, without explanation, it shifted to my right. Along the way, I encountered the usual series of roadblocks. At one, a policeman permitted me to walk in one direction but not the other. "A one way street to human traffic," I remarked. "That could only happen in Hero." Comically, he snapped his fingers to rush me along.

Closer to the obelisk, I found the rally to deliver everything promised in the pamphlet, and more. It featured not only its share of megaphones, banners, and speeches to inspire the crowd, but also children bedecked in capes and painted faces. From a gridlock of street carts, vendors sold shaved ice cones in assortments of flavors—purple, blue, or red. I couldn't tell if I was at a protest rally—or at the circus. But what most caught my attention were the slogans chanted by squads of rabble raisers cruising the turf in pickup trucks. The spontaneous eruption of riots was beginning to show an invisible, organizing hand. But to what end? Posing this question to one of the rally's speakers, I was put on the spot in return. "You're him," he said, recognizing the name on my press ID card, "the one who writes the articles about the corpses." I wasn't sure how to feel about my newfound fame. But as the activist attempted to answer my question, or really just recapitulate his speech, I began to recognize how all points led back to a common source—and the source was me. "Two corpses were at large in Hero," my latest article pointed out, then simply presented the facts. I don't know that I foresaw how, in the street, the implication alone would be taken for just that—a fact. It was clear that from the rally emerged a new consensus. Since the day rioters discovered the Commander's body missing from the morgue, the public had no doubt it was The Authority who took it. Thanks to me, they now suspected the corpse had then been dumped into an unmarked pauper's grave. In Hero, one cannot underestimate the grievous nature of the insult.

I guess this is what Pea Nuts meant by "responsible journalism"—or its alternative, the irresponsible kind. As much as I hate to admit it, he may have had a point. Either way, it seemed to implicate me in some irreversible way, leading me to wonder if, in the body politic, I had contributed my very own stem cell. In horror, I projected its growth into the shape of the mouth, learning to swallow and spit, and ultimately, to drown in the salt of the tide.

CHAPTER SEVEN

WINDOW

CONDEMNED BUILDING

PRESS ROOM, Hero — I said, "Good luck writing your condemned building"—and I had meant it sincerely, whether or not Zoey took it that way.

"Good luck writing the war," she rebounded, "Hotshot."

I don't know why Zoey hates me so much—unless it goes back to the award I once got from the International Unified Press. But that happened so long ago, and I have not cared to repeat the performance that earned me acclaim as "Reporter of the Year." Not only did I fail to deliver an encore, I did better. I packed my stuff and left—as in, quit out of Hero. In the end, all "Reporter of the Year," did was make me a glorified word jock, though Pea Nuts prefers to say, "dumb writer—in a war zone."

I can only guess that Zoey felt restricted by Lifestyles—having covered more than her fair share of "ditsy stories" (which she also refers to as "the bizarre pets and haunted house chronicles"). Engrossing as the articles may be to her readers, they must seem small consolation for the serious career that might have been. Lately, however, I'd been noticing Zoey throw herself into Lifestyles with a newfound zeal. She got religion, she said, in the mission to save one of Hero's oldest architectural treasures. Namely, it was to chronicle the citizens' campaign to save the ancient soap factory from seizure and demolition by bureaucrats. Recently adding it to their list of condemned properties, "the bureaucrats have declared it a fire hazard, and would you believe, a rebel safe house?" Zoey balked. "What kind of rebels take over a building next door to a police station?"

Ballsy ones, I imagined. It turned out that just months ago, that was exactly what happened. Of course, as soon as the words "rebel" and "siege" were mentioned, the topic spilled over into my territory. Moreover, Sophi's prior mention of the soap factory in connection with the Commander had already stoked my curiosity. So, armed with additional background from Zoey, I decided it was time to pay the unlikely fortress a visit.

Its mortar structure is less than spectacular to the eye—there being more glorious architectural achievements in Hero. This did not stop The Board of Heroaen Antiquities (a volunteer organization) from proclaiming the two thousand year old factory an official historic site. I suspect this has as much to do with the building's association with soap—a celebrated local tradition—than with its age or physical form. And yet, in spite of this, the factory has an understated quality that makes it quintessentially Heroaen—punished by nature's elements, neglected by human industry, and on the verge of being abandoned by time.

Appropriately enough, this being Hero, the first thing I saw there was a protest. Waving yet another fleet of signs, the picketers bore an eerie resemblance to the demonstrators of yesterday's rally. But they differed dramatically in purpose. Rather than to recoup the remains of the dead man, the preoccupation of today's group was to preserve the thing that had been precious to him during his life. Oddly enough, when I asked one of the demonstrators what she thought of the Commander's devotion to the soap factory, she replied absently, "I had no idea what he, or his rebels, had to do with the building—unless you mean the siege. Well, you know, that happened *a while ago*." I guess, with all that happens in Hero, she had reason to consider even last season's events out-dated news. Further, she seemed to regard the incident as anti-climactic, especially since, after a few days, the army came and "broke it up." As co-chair of The Board of Heroaen Antiquities, she was far more concerned with the fate of the factory which, luckily, suffered minimal damage in the storming of the rebels. To her dismay, however, The Authority cited the siege as just cause to take over the building—preventing rebels from using it as a potential headquarters, I suppose.

Today, it is thoroughly cordoned off with tape and official signs warning against trespassers. "No one has been through here," the co-chair attested, "except for the couple who appeared to be squatters. A tall, well-built man—and a girl." Squeezed by economic hardship, the homeless increasingly take shelter in abandoned buildings—even condemned ones. "They moved with the ease of shadows, close together, like twin planes on the narrow strip of a runway. The poor souls, to be adrift," she said. "And yet, they looked very romantic."

RUMORS

"In Hero, we have a saying," Hektor quoted. "'All it takes is a good strong wind to blow over a lie.' Because, you see, a lie is weightless. It is hollow in the center."

I told him I have heard the proverb.

"Then maybe you can understand this. When you have lived long enough in Hero, you learn that a lie is a very weak thing. Rumor? That's something different. To stop a rumor would take *a great deal more than the wind*."

For a change, we were not talking about the political wind.

IT IS DIFFICULT to say exactly when Antigone started talking—or why. But I have since wondered whether it was simply to tell me her stark memory of a dream that had not even been her own. For, in spite of the informal introduction provided by her sister, the early days of our acquaintance were tentative. Having glimpsed me on a number of occasions, Antigone displayed a curiosity without desire to risk actual contact—regarding me with a studied, even cautious, tolerance. And when by chance I'd see her, the presence was always momentary. Darting with the grace and ease of a deer, Antigone proved every bit as elusive as Sophi implied.

I finally caught up with her, as I suspected I would, curled up with a book at the base of her tree. It was there, in the vacant lot across from the morgue, that we conducted our first conversation. It would lead, among other things, to a description of her earliest impression of the Commander. "Two men came to the door in the night," she recalled, "and asked if they could sleep on the floor of the parlor." Alarmed by the sounds of their snoring, Antigone stayed up all night, "just to watch them." Paying special attention to the Commander, she observed that "he was gripped in the fever of a dream."

That's when, insensitively, I decided to open the subject. "I have heard something," I began, "and I don't know whether to believe it. But it seems that, as a rumor, it has wrought a good deal of damage."

"Well, people say things when they don't have any real way of knowing."

"But you have an idea of what I am talking about."

"Maybe," she shrugged, followed by a noncommittal, "I don't know."

"You and the Commander…"

Antigone disrupted my question by turning her back, but I persisted.

"People say that you and he spent some time together in the weeks before his death."

"Well, it was spring."

"That's right, it was."

"We had time."

She shrugged in an unconvincing effort to be dismissive. I continued.

"People thought that, perhaps, you had feelings for each other, and that this created... problems."

"Problems," Antigone said, picking up the trail of my statement. But she had done so with irony, half with laugh. I had detected it only by the tiny uplift of her shoulders, and the echo of a sigh. I was no longer certain I wanted to proceed, but decided to do so anyway.

"After all, you had promised to marry another man."

"Hektor," she affirmed. "He is away now."

"Yes, I know him. Many times, I have been up to the prison."

I felt the word "prison" stick in the air—like a poison arrow. And then, I saw the contraction of her shoulders followed by a shrinking of elbows.

"I am sorry to ask," I pressed, "but what was your relationship with the Commander?"

As I watched her effort to compact into a ball, I began to regret my cruelty.

"You don't have to talk about it if you don't want to," I relented.

Antigone turned. To my surprise, she unfolded like the petals of a flower. Then openly, and without a trace of inhibition, she revealed the answer.

"We made soap."

I might have guessed she'd say that.

FACTORY

The cavernous room was lit, and only sparsely, by a hole cut directly into the stone of the wall, a short distance below the ceiling. From the high, arched window, a diffuse white light spilled in, misting her face and hair. With quiet and deliberate intent, Antigone worked the metal shears he had given her.

She used them to clip the large sheets of parchment paper into squares, just large enough to wrap a single, finished bar. Wrapping was to happen in the final stages—after the pouring, the cutting, and the curing. The curing stage alone would last ten days. At that time, perhaps, she would come again to the lofty room lit by a single window. And she would sit on the little elm wood bench to fold each soap into a square of parchment paper, tie it with string, and pack it into a crate to be transported to the market.

For the moment, she stretched a toe. Sighing a little, she tried concentrating on the paper, the squeaking of the steel blades, the clamping and loosening of her fingers on the wooden handles. But, as before, her eyes wandered from the shears and the lines that she was cutting, toward the center of the floor where he stood above the iron pots set over open flames. She memorized him stirring. Many hours later, recalling that moment, her eyes would fill up with the sight of his rhythmic labors, his scarred hands wielding the enormous stick in steady circles. And in that recollection, the air would again be infused with the heavy aroma of olive oil and soot. Towards sundown, when the alchemy of heat, water, oil, and wood ash was completed, he held the pots, one after the other, over a shallow depression carved into the floor. Into the immense mold he tipped the pots, pouring quickly without splashing, flooding the floor in a sea of soap.

AMONG THE RUINS

Summer evenings in Hero are about waiting for a breeze. With screenless windows flung open, I lay prostrate on the cot in the smoldering heat, and couldn't stop thinking about Sophi. My attempts not to were useless, so more and more I just gave in. She might as well have been in the room with me; she had become an immovable part of the space. Whether or not she knew it, Sophi was now in the labyrinth—along with me.

The thing to know about Sophi and spaces is that every square inch of her longs for a home of her own. She has described it to me in great detail, to the point where I can see it as it truly exists. The home is not grand, but it is definitely spacious. I know this because the measurement begins in Sophi's heart, where she has already scaled it to perfection. There are the oblong rooms adjacent to the round ones; and the rooms whose shapes are as intricate as paper cutouts layered carefully on top of one another. Like her spaces, Sophi's imagination has no bounds. But mostly, Sophi's home is about the doorways. Plentiful and inviting, they lead to ever more generous spaces on the inside. And yet, whenever I have been in Sophi's home—the actual one—I am struck by the smallness of the space. There was another thing, too, that didn't fit right. Whenever I have been in Sophi's home, I knew that I was where I was not because of the size the rooms, but because of the smells. I now know that Sophi bakes bread in order to fill her home with the aroma of thyme; but to this day, I have never seen Sophi eat the bread.

At Rix, too, her plate of bread lay untouched beside her vessel of coffee. And, while I have a nervous habit of rapping my knuckles against the table, she watched me.

"You're an interesting man, James," she observed.

My rapping picked up a beat.

"In what way?" I returned.

"In the way that you are different from so many of the men here, and yet the same." After pausing to relish the hold she had taken on my curiosity (and my psyche), she explained. "You seem forever to be fighting a war—if not with an enemy, then with yourself." She sighed, "Such a life of punishment." Smiling sweetly, she'd come out hitting hard—and unerringly close to the truth.

"Maybe you're right," I confessed. "I'm a writer. And writing is an unmerciful act—if you are going to be honest."

"Unmerciful?" she questioned.

"Like a pair of fists," I said, "without the gloves."

I had thrown that statement playfully, because it is an image I associate so strongly with the fighters of Hero we'd been talking about.

"Oh," she affirmed with a nod of her head. With a sudden gesture, Sophi covered my hands with her own, spreading her supple fingers over the tense, protruding knuckles I had anchored to the table like two rocks. I had stopped rapping my fists—but was clenching them. "Do you mean these?" she asked.

"No, these," I corrected, abruptly flipping and cupping her small hands into mine. She had always been the one to hit the harder. But caught off guard, Sophi softened, tucking her fingers back into the folds of her lap.

"Writing can be unforgiving," I rejoined, "but it has taught me a lesson."

"That it's not always possible to be the nice guy?"

"It's more like…sometimes you have to *take* before you can give back," I told her.

"Maybe that depends on what you're taking," she said. Then, unsparingly, "Why are you so interested in Hero?"

"I don't know."

"For a man who is always asking questions, you rarely like to answer them."

"Maybe I came looking for trouble," I replied.

And from the first day of knocking on her door, I had seen it coming. In my throat I sensed a sudden tightness, and in my chest, the beginning pangs of a disturbance. But neither succeeded in preventing me from taking it on. At nightfall, we haunted Sophi's streets like a pair of sleepwalkers, winding our way back to the spareness of my room. Our hands laced together like a brand new pair of fighters' gloves—too tight and untested, perhaps, yet knotted by faith coupled with the clenching of our fists. After our bout of love (or with it), Sophi fell into the most easy and delicate sleep that I have ever seen. I stayed awake, resting my eyes on the soft dips and rises of her back, curves that filled and ebbed with every effortless breath. I know this is how Hero must have looked at its purest beginning, and I wanted to stretch out on the bareness of that terrain—forever.

BATH

In the precarious balance between longing and struggle, the Commander, too, had been on the edge of losing his footing.

His affliction became apparent in the long hours he'd spend alone in the condemned factory where he deposited his scant belongings. With a perplexity bordering on disbelief, his Lieutenant later told me, "He slept there, as if he had moved in. I couldn't understand it. In the past we sought shelter in the homes of our supporters, and never stayed too long in one place. This helped us avoid being captured." Abruptly and without explanation, the Commander abandoned the precaution. "It was as if he left the war overnight," the Lieutenant explained—sounding abandoned, himself. "From that point onward, I saw that I was on my own." According to the Lieutenant, the Commander's behavior grew even stranger late in spring. "I'd look for him all over the city, only to find him in the factory among the barrels. He'd be sitting and staring at the stacks of soap, with a faraway look that was not about the war, or fighting. Over and over, he would point to the stacks and say, 'We made those.' What is that but the sign of a sick man?"

I suppose that, stricken, the Commander would conjure up the image of Antigone seated on the elm wood bench, patiently applying the blades of the scissors to the unruly sheets of waxen paper, cutting them into perfect little squares. No stretch of security tape, or repeated postings of No Trespass signs, had been enough to prevent them from entering a space that had really been theirs, had belonged to them by an inalienable right. It was there, inside the factory walls, that the girl had given herself over completely, and with an openness so perfect, it could only have been called faith. He had never known anything so strong in life. In her eyes, he reclaimed the vision of lost things, and saw them as they were supposed to be—haunting and distant and new. Hour after hour they worked under that spell, entranced by the heat of the fire and of their bodies close together. At the finish, they saw that they had revived the old formula and made a soap that, with its vapors and the sticky weight of it, at once sloughed away the scaly, caked mass of the least accounted for sins.

ROOM WITH A VIEW

The sweet voice said, "Tell the truth, James."

"I'm trying," I told her, but with a steadiness that seemed dishonest—if only because it betrayed no terror. Perhaps it should have. I had no idea whether I was confiding or confessing…when out it came. "I loved somebody once."

She mused on the information.

"Did it make you happy?"

"In the end, I was happy she finally found what she needed—and it wasn't me."

I then dribbled on about how happiness is relative. Happiness is what you imagine it to be…

"Tell the truth, James," my companion persisted.

In the end, I gave in to the seductive repetition of the question.

"The truth is, we both know I will never belong to Hero."

"That's a lie," she said. "Hero already owns you."

"Okay, then. It doesn't change the fact that I'm only passing through. But you…"

I hesitated, considering every angle of deflection, before accepting that I had little choice but to be honest.

"You, Sophi, will never want to leave."

She lifted her head from the crook of my arm, strafing me with thoughts I could not begin to interpret. Then she moved to the wall. I watched as she pulled the linen dress over the curve of her shoulders, passing her hands over the length of it to smooth out the wrinkles. Barefoot, she stepped idly toward the window, where sunlight was beginning to fully penetrate the room. Beyond the window and the profile of Sophi looking out, I saw, for the first time, the hidden glory of the city—spread across the sooty horizon of factory rooftops.

CHAPTER EIGHT

REDEMPTION LOST

SLEEP

OLD CITY, Hero — On the night she watched over him in the parlor, Antigone could not know the cause, or source, of the Commander's feverish dream. She knew only that he—a stranger—had been carried into her home in the middle of the night, and upon the shoulders of a second man she likewise had never seen.

She did observe that, thrashing about on the floor, the stranger had the look of a man caught in an overpowering current; and she feared that, at any instant, he may drown. She does remember that the room was dark. And she did see that the blanket she'd thrown over him had become wet, but assumed it was with the brackish moisture of his fever. In the dark, and in all innocence, Antigone saw the blanket soaked in a mixture of sweat and water. She did not see the swimmer awash in the thicker substance that was his blood.

In hindsight, it appears that blindness was the first thing the Commander and the girl had shared. And while he would recover from his wounds (as he had on all previous occasions), the real danger was his blindness. Like Antigone failing to see the blood upon his blanket, the Commander detected no trace of the betrayal seeping slowly into the heart of his Lieutenant. In the end, it was this oversight that would prove fatal.

As blindnesses go, it is an easy one to envision. As boys, the pair had met in prison, their cells placed side-by-side. Growing up, they became as close as brothers. For a time, they even felt they had no family except each other.

Still, while thinking of his family, it must have seemed to the Commander a particularly poignant failure to have let the ancestral soap factory slip back out of his hands. However valiant the effort, he and his fighters had reclaimed and held it for a mere matter of days. Then, narrowly escaping the raid that followed, it was again the Lieutenant who had pulled him from the wreckage, patched his wounds up, and procured for them both one more floor to sleep on. It was the Lieutenant who made it possible for the war to continue.

THREE MEN

But on the day the Commander, Lieutenant, and Hektor barricaded themselves inside the walls of the factory, all knew that the stand—largely symbolic—would be their last. Like any good paradox, it only makes sense if you know how they got there.

Consider three men joined in youth by the circumstance they called prison. For a time, they became separated—at least one of them did—only to be reunited by the unremitting factor we can only call Fate. If you can keep that much straight, Hektor does a nice job filling in the rest.

"Early on, we'd met in the Program," he began (citing prison-speak for boxing). Then, he smiled. "In Hero, we say hell has its perks."

Some even call it redemption.

The Program was a chance to fight with fists instead of bombs—and actually win. It was glory of a sort—at once carved, chiseled, and gouged from the pit of the wasteland. Of the young Commander, Hektor beamed, "he had Local Spirit"—Hero-speak for whatever you'd guess. I like to call it Hope-Taped-Tight-Inside-a-Core-of-Rage. In any case, it is nothing short of a force.

"Being a year or so older, naturally I was a senior to the other two. But hell has its own rules—and neither nature or seniority count among them; result being, they both got sprung before I did."

Repeatedly denied parole, Hektor's own youth continued to wither inside prison walls. Meanwhile, "On the outside, those boys were busy making legends of themselves."

They called each other rebels, forging loyalty in a mixture of dirt and blood. Sleeping in cave hideouts was the dirt part. The blood of it flowed each time they dragged each other from the debris of another ambush. They adopted official war names which, for fun, they occasionally interchanged. From the era of caves, they emerged bearing the titles of Commander and Lieutenant; deciding that, for the time remaining, that's how they wished to be known in the world. "We had remarkable success," the Lieutenant recounted proudly.

It was true—they had made a formidable rebellion, incited fear and contempt in their enemies, and were embraced in their neighborhoods as history's long-lost princes. But for the duo's leader, there was a necessary limit to the fun. "Over time, his thinking began going its own way," the Lieutenant reported. "In the final year, he decided the war was useless—that it hadn't got us any real gain. 'We've done enough,' he'd say, and I could see the future in his eyes. After the losing factory, the war was just about over for him." Mixing bemusement and disgust, the Lieutenant added, "It was as if he had lost his love."

Hektor was less romantic about his part in the effort. "I went along with him," he recalled of the Commander, "for foolish reasons. And yet, they were my reasons."

"Did they have to do with Local Spirit?" I ventured.

"Perhaps," Hektor conceded; "more importantly, he asked."

It had been an effortless recruitment—if less than prudent. "Going in, my heart was torn," Hektor confided. "We knew we were going to be outnumbered. From the start, I didn't go for victory, but for the brothers. Even so, I worried for the future. I'd made promises."

Not least was to the girl he was waiting to marry.

When Security Forces stormed the building, the Commander pushed him through a window into the fetid alley. "That was meant to save me," Hektor explained, "but instead, it burned. Through tears of shame, I cried, 'why?'

"He just said, 'promises.'"

CHAPTER NINE

ORDINARY LIVES

A DAY IN THE LIFE

OLD CITY, Hero — I don't know how sincere the envy, but Zoey had been right about one thing. I do get to spend my day chasing dead bodies. But for a man who earns his living from war zones, it's odd that such a privilege ever came as a surprise. Moreover, I might have predicted how quickly my writing of the war would turn into the story of the corpses—and the plural is no mistake; they are multiplying. To be exact, the number has doubled—as in, a pair of dead men—not even counting the unidentified one plundered from the pauper's grave. It is a duo, rather, that derives from actual, verifiable bodies.

From the outset, I couldn't dismiss as coincidence that the Commander and Lieutenant died within weeks of one another. But I was now reminded that every investigation has a natural starting point. This being Hero, the inversion principle at once kicked in—endings make the best beginnings. So I set out to reconstruct what each of the dead men was doing on the last day of his living. Neither one forecasting his fate, the Commander and Lieutenant each went about his normal activities—even as the rest of the world glimpsed his doom.

From his mother's house, the Commander stepped out to the quiet street just at the verge of daybreak. Glancing to the right and left, he advanced briskly toward the alley just a few paces away. "He'd always been an early riser," reported a neighbor, "and he always took that shortcut, even from the time he was a boy." The lady would be the last to see the Commander as he departed the house of his mother—and the sighting had caused her surprise. "These days, our sons seldom come home. They're not bad boys, you understand. It's just the business." Seeking clarity, I'd asked, "The business of rebellion?" She sniffed, "Well, I don't mean the selling of shoes." She then recalled a "strange feeling" about her neighbor's son's visit but, citing a preoccupation with chores, had ignored the augury. Backing away from the window, the lady left the Commander to embark on his circuitous path.

It would lead from the house of his mother past an array of familiar, dilapidated doorways—including the entrance to the factory where a stone plaque still bore his family's name. Even then, the Commander walked on without interest. Instead, he sought the door that, during a previous homecoming, had been the first to open. "My son was still a boy when the authorities took him—and not given back until he was fully a man," his father informed. "To young men, freedom comes as a shock." Returning, the native son discovered that the pieces of his world had fractured and shifted. In the street, the city's youth hovered in alleys, collecting beneath the lamp posts; but he no longer fit among them. Yet, within a short time—and despite the maturity of his will—like them, he became waylaid.

From the second floor of a white-washed, well-kept building, a woman in yellow peered out. Bashfully, perhaps, the young man returned her gaze. Then, slipping both hands into rumpled trouser pockets, he pulled them out again—producing only the lint. At the door (where she'd been able to assess the situation more fully), the woman sighed, "Well, it's not always the money that chooses."

Upstairs, he met a room cluttered with objects, some cheap and some expensive, with many more propped up inside half open boxes—either the gifts of lovers, or the spoils of war. He regarded them with a mild astonishment. "Men pay me to take their loneliness," she explained, "as if I stand there on the beach with a net to catch it, and love is nothing more than a slippery kind of fish." With a seagull laugh, she pulled him down into the water, where they held hands while rolling in the tide. Forgetting air, they came under the impression that they had drowned. It took the salty spray from her lips to revive him.

"How was my fish?" he inquired, "or, as you say, my loneliness?"

"My poor man," she sighed. "It is deeper and wider than the ocean."

MEETING A FRIEND

On the morning his assassins were preparing to kill him, the Commander again left his mother's house to cross the matrix of alleys threading past numerous doorways. Detecting his approach from her upstairs window, the woman in yellow started descending the stairwell—as she always had—to let him in without his having to knock. Never had he needed to announce his arrival because, since the beginning of their acquaintance, she'd been able to sense in advance that he was coming.

But on that morning, she sensed a different purpose in the visit. Without revealing the reason, he'd simply searched the parlor and bedroom—sliding out drawers, turning over cushions, and scrutinizing apparently harmless objects. At length, he asked if she had seen his field coat—"the faded green one with a misshapen patch at the sleeve." Recalling that the garment had been stained by coffee, she disclosed, "I thought best to send it out with the laundry." His alarm made sense only later, days later, when the laundry service returned the field coat. Fishing a cartridge out of the pocket, she realized that "I was holding the last of his bullets." But the significance of the discovery still perplexed her. Before leaving her that final morning, "he had talked about meeting a friend." Under the circumstances, there seemed little reason to anticipate danger; and in fact, he may not have.

"I WAS NOT PLANNING for a duel," Hektor explained, "but a civil discussion." With carefully measured words, he thus composed the letter he then personally passed to the Lieutenant as they stood, incognito, under the ruins of an unspecified, crumbling bridge (in Hero, there are numerous examples of this structure). There, the Lieutenant agreed to deliver the message into the hands of the Commander, and presumably did so later that day. The need for discretion was simple. "At that time, I was just returning from the caves," Hektor explained. After narrowly escaping the raid of the soap factory, he had survived the spring by hiding in the mountains. Returning meant that, like his comrades, he had acquired official fugitive status. Under the circumstances, arranging to meet the Commander was no easy matter. It was necessary to select a spot where the two men might connect in secret and at the specified hour. "Don't worry," the Lieutenant guaranteed. "The location will be perfectly safe."

BITTER COFFEE

"Ideals make us pathetic," the Lieutenant stated. "They don't make us wrong." As I watched him nervously swirl the grinds at the bottom of his coffee, his remark struck me as one of the hardest-learned lessons in Hero. Frankly, I don't draw from it all that much comfort. I wonder if, in the end, it brought him any.

It so happened that on the morning of the day that the mob would be waiting to kill him, the Lieutenant had arranged to meet me for breakfast. Once again, I'd been entirely passive in the solicitation of the interview—and was equally unsuspecting. All I'd really done was pick up the phone. In a tense but self-assured voice, the Lieutenant baited me from my desk with the prospect of "Hero's hottest tip." He would disclose it in person, he said, if I would agree to meet him at a nearby hole-in-the-wall cafe. I made it there in what felt like the world's fastest hundred yard dash. As free opportunities go, however, my faith (and exertion) were only partially rewarded. Within less than half an hour, the Lieutenant cut our talk short, irritated by the rising din of the other diners. "Noise gives me a headache," he complained, "and the coffee here is too bitter for my taste."

I stayed behind and finished my eggs, chewing over no more profound a notion than that he'd been right about the coffee. Only later did I realize how right he'd also been about the infallibility of men's ideals (at least, their lack of wrongness). I suppose it was with an incorruptible sense of rightness that the Lieutenant had met a pair of secret agents on the eve of the assassination of the Commander. "I gave them a time and place to find the man they wanted," the Lieutenant confessed, "but they were only supposed to arrest him." Naïvely or not, he genuinely seemed to have believed it.

It's difficult knowing what to believe anymore. Reality these days—or one's sense of it—readily shifts with the wind. Along with it goes one's confidence in either the stability, or shakeability, of the world. In Hero, the experience tends toward shaky—not least so in the political realm. Ask any resident here what they think of the ongoing dialogue between rebel factions and the state to resolve the conflict, and reactions will range from cautious optimism to fatal disgust—depending on how their day is going; or rather, the direction and force of the wind.

Three years ago, it blew in like a jet stream, whipping about something so new and extraordinary that we'd all been at a loss of what to call it—though at the time, it had felt like hope. Eventually, the phenomenon acquired the official name, "Peace Summits," an internationally sponsored movement heavily touted by the press. But for Heroaens, the ensuing period fell far short of actual peace. Reconciliations made on paper never fully—or honestly—addressed the problems of real people. The lull in violence lasted a brief two years. Then, with patience worn and promises broken, the rebel factions again took up their arms. Looking back, however, many Heroaens regard the diplomatic efforts of that era as not entirely bleak. At least for a time, some had embraced the glimmer of what might be possible. Shortly before leaving the Heroaen bureau, I had spoken to one such optimist.

"THE POOR do not have armies," I quoted him saying. "We have *guerrillas*—in Hero, we say 'fighters.' In the papers, this has been called a guerilla war. People say that our tactics are dirty. Have you ever known a war that was clean?" he challenged. "In the end, we will win this dirty war. They know it, and we know it. What remains to be seen is how long it will take us, and how severe the losses will be." With emphatic gestures, the celebrated rebel expressed with his hands that which was concealed by the hood over his face. His voice took on the soft rasp of a philosopher. "You see, a poor man fights with *will* as his greatest weapon. Thus, he can only succeed as far as he can persevere. When the other side grows weary of his own suffering, the fighter will win. In the world, we have seen that such wars are won by the side that is able to suffer more. And harder. And longer. This is the side which knows, in the heart, that it is right."

But as unwavering as he remained in the ultimate objective, he hinted at his own internal debate when, refilling our vessels of coffee, he steered us in a new, lately controversial, direction.

"Among the factions there has been disagreement regarding some tactics," he began. "For my part, I am against the targeting of civilians."

"On moral grounds?" I suggested.

"Of course, it is indefensible," he returned, then more rhetorically, "But aren't we talking about a war?"

"On what basis, then?"

"Because tactically, it is a mistake. It harms the ordinary people, while the rich remain secure in their houses—making the decisions. There are those among us who say that striking the person on the street puts pressure on the enemy in his fortress; that over time, this wears him down. From what I have seen, it only gives him the excuse to hit us harder. As a result, we harm ourselves."

Without meaning to sound facetious, I asked, "Does that make you feel picked on?"

"Who in this world isn't picked on? Baby seals are picked on."

"Baby seals don't lead insurrections," I pointed out.

"Is that what this is? And to think, in Hero we were calling it a war."

"Have it your way—a war."

"The war has taught me there are no aggressors. Only victims. Nobody wins and everybody loses."

For the moment, I was tempted to interpret his remark as conciliatory, a tone that was later retracted when I asked him, "Is it necessary to hate the enemy in order to fight him?" After a thoughtful pause, he said, "Maybe you should ask that to my colleague." He then nodded to the gunman at the window, who supplied, "Well, the hating can only help." And the two men laughed. The absurd innocence of my question seemed to delight them both. Afterwards, more seriously, the gunman proposed, "Imagine that Hero is a contest of sport. Then ask me again, 'is it necessary to hate the opponent in order to fight him?' There is only one answer, 'So long as the objective is to win.'"

Reconsidering, the masked speaker simply redirected the question. "I don't know about hate," he said, "but I know about suffering. It is enough that my enemy is responsible for my suffering. To throw him off is my right. Besides," he added casually, "it is the intention of my will." With the same cool conviction, he clicked a new cartridge into the chamber of his pistol. No further emphasis was required. Throughout the lengthy interview, I had picked up a rather mixed measure. And yet, regardless of the contradictions, I had gleaned from the rebel leader more than a casual hint of his position. "If they say 'peace,' then let them mean it," he said, adding firmly, "That, too, is my intention."

It was also the wedge in a growing rift with his closest comrade. Cast as unwitting combatants, they were already set to square off in a war about nothing—out of which emerge no victors. In the future, that would become apparent. For the moment, exchanging dark flashes of humor, the two men were not even aware of sitting in the same room, espousing the same doomed causes.

RECALL

It would take me three years to make the connection between the two men and the rush of present events—sparked by the Lieutenant's reminder that one long ago afternoon, he had already had met me. "I can see you have forgotten," he said, smiling over the rim of his mug of bitter coffee. "I was the one without the mask." When the realization finally hit, it met my head with the full force of a well-aimed rock (the real thing, as in, launched from Hero).

Like a prophecy, or a misdirected dream, I understood how it all had happened....three years ago, in an unidentifiable secluded apartment, the masked man speaking while the other, unconcealed, perched in silence at the sill of the window... most of all, I remembered then, as now, the endless steaming vessels of coffee...So came my recognition that the man I'd seen pulled from the drawer of the morgue was none other than the once-masked rebel, his face revealed at last.

THE LIEUTENANT grimaced over the poor flavor of his brew. I could only agree. The coffee was not up to standard. Taking advantage of the example, he went on to express chagrin about the plummeting quality of life in general, which, predictably, turned into a political harangue against Hero's foreign oppressors. But when I pointed out the obvious dangers of being perceived in the street as a collaborator, the Lieutenant's reaction was the only surprise. "Collaborator?" he repeated with disgust. "Only for the good of the movement, could I have done it. Not one of them was as close to him as I was. No one saw—as I did—how he stopped believing. This hurt the cause, made weak what we were saying. And still, he was to me, a brother. We fought together our whole lives. So what of the people, as you say, in the street? On behalf of them, I fed him to the dogs." He paused in exasperation. "If they want to call me 'collaborator,'—let them go to the dogs."

It seemed a bewildering statement coming from one who had sacrificed everything to the war—including life and brotherhood; unless, of course, it was the scream of a man buckling under the weight of his ideals.

THE SOLACE

Just like a sea ship, a house in Hero can be given a name. She is "The Solace," and nowhere is Old Hero more evident than on the street where Solace lives. Overshadowed by the picketers' campaign to save the neighboring soap factory, The Solace is yet a formidable presence. But, unlike the retired factory, she is valued less for her architecture than for the continuing viability of her service, best explained by the inscription on the step of the door. It reads, "Dedicated to the art of forgetting," followed by a convincingly earnest "Welcome." Structures like The Solace also testify to the earliest settling of the town. Simply put, Forget Houses predated the rival technologies of theaters, coliseums, and TV sets. While all shared the business of entertainment, The Solace continues to survive them all, for the simple reason that none supplanted the need that Forget Houses proved so good at addressing. That is men's longing for amnesia—a promised, if momentary, escape from the prisons of their bodies. "We take in jailbirds," a resident told me, "that's why we're here." In the street, The Solace is said to be more than a vessel; that she is a receptacle for Hero's sad love. Those living inside it prefer to call it the "trash can." I asked the resident if she thought people would ever picket to save her building—if it came to that. "I think there is no need to worry," she reassured me. "When the sands have blown away, only The Solace will be left here standing."

BATTLES OF LOVE

Prompted to describe her most notable client, the woman in yellow recalled, "He had black eyes, darker than the bottom of the sea. You could never see entirely what was in them." In actuality, the eyes were brown. Every Heroaen is a poet, of course, and residents of The Solace are no exception. Moreover, the enigma of that man was deepened by the fact that she has never traveled far enough from Hero to reach the coastline. But no matter how remote or unattainable, the ocean was the image she had chosen. Whipping out my notebook, I gratefully committed her words to ink. That seemed to please her and she continued, revealing in the next few statements that her name was Palome, a word that, in the Heroaen language, means "dove" (though why not seagull? I thought it better not to ask). In any case, had she soared out of a fairy tale, Dove could not have better fit the role of damsel-trapped-in-tower. She was classic. And I had found her, like I always do, on the fly. That is how one discovers things in Hero. To be exact, it was more like she was the one discovering me—having spotted my presence from her lofty window. Locating my way by its proximity to the soap factory, I had hardly appeared on her street by accident, but had gone there looking for her. Momentarily, however, she embarrassingly misread my intentions when I knocked on her

door (she was, after all, a woman of business). I told her I had
not come as a client, but as a journalist collecting information
about the slain commander. Graciously, Palome exaggerated
her disappointment (I think I was the one embarrassed). In any
case, we got down to business—not hers, but mine.

"I am told you had some association with the rebel," I
began.

"The Commander," she affirmed. "Yes, I knew him."

Thereafter, she referred to her former lover more specifically
by his nom de guerre, the word that in her language means
"Hero." I proceeded to run down a list of questions, the kind
one typically asks with the objective of profiling a man. But
they had to do with his beliefs, his politics, and his leadership—
details which did not seem to interest her. Accordingly, I pushed
onto the more intimate subject of his habits and manners.
Succinctly, she replied, "There was nothing fancy about him."
With some thought, she added, "He kept few possessions."

"I understand," I nodded.

"Don't be mistaken," Palome corrected. "He preferred the
spareness." She seemed to regard that as a peculiar aspect of
his nature. Looking around the ornate parlor, I could see her
bewilderment. Apparently, she herself had no qualms about
reaping the material rewards of her chosen work. Shrugging,
she added, "Beside that, he was a private person, somewhat
uncomfortable around people. Most of all, he knew the secret
to happiness. He'd tell me, 'It is very simple. Life doesn't owe
us a thing.'" Reflecting, she concluded, "In some ways, he was
a very hard man."

"And yet, you were in love with him?" I inquired bluntly. It
seemed an odd question to put to a professional woman.

"Perhaps," she agreed, but with the flippancy of one who
is saying very little. "In this work, one is in love all the time.
Seldom does it turn out to be real; and always, it is fleeting. I
think I am not so much a professional lover as a dreamer. In the
end, that makes me a fool."

"For dreaming?" I asked.

"For wanting to be loved," she corrected. "Isn't it stupid?"

I guess only the Commander would have known how he would answer. A behavioral scientist, however, once asserted that love is nothing more than the impulse of life grappling with its own extinction. When I told Palome that, she smiled. "Men fear love more than they fear death," she said. Equally enlightening was her suggestion that love is an untimely seizure of panic, its aftershock, and the apologies later. I supply no theory of my own, except the observation that men appeal to logic for explanations they can live with—so long as we all agree on the story. To us, what matters is the potency of the dream.

"RETURNING FROM the caves, I felt I owed him," Hektor acknowledged. "But what does a man say to another who saves his life, then hopes to steal his girlfriend?" In the alley location they agreed on, the two fugitives brooded over their dilemma and were able, for the moment, to draw conclusion. "We agreed that love is a disorder," said Hektor, sharing this dismal understanding, if not forgiveness, with the Commander just moments before the headlights of a vehicle beamed bright. "It came rolling at us slowly. All at once, that looked suspicious. Getting closer, the lights of the car went dim...At first, I wondered which of us they came for. But then, our eyes met. It was as if he knew the answer."

Of all recollections of the Commander that I've gathered, none have failed to mention that mercurial sad quality. I'd even glimpsed it once myself—in the twin globes peering out at me from the slits of a mask. It occurs to me, though only now, to detect in Hektor's statement the echo of an earlier conversation—one by chance I'd conducted with a soldier at the morgue. Speaking in anonymity, he had described to me the calmness of a blindfolded man he had dreamed. Had the unidentified man resembled the Commander, the soldier would have been right in his interpretation of his own reverie. Both men, it seems, shared a gift for previewing their fates.

Of that, Hektor seemed firm in his conviction. I, on the other hand, had not been there—and cannot comment on the Commander's precise reaction. Indeed, the full events of that night will forever elude me. I can only amass what remains in the memories of those present at the scene. To my dismay, scant information can be gleaned from the eyewitness statements. At Rix, an assembly of late night diners saw him dash past the window along the pane that faces Canary Boulevard. But all were strangers who, never having met the Commander, registered no recognition. (Oddly enough, all were aware of his celebrity and, if prompted, could recite stories of his military exploits.) Further along the street, an additional six people reported hearing an untimely rapping on their doors. That number included the apothecary who, in the habit of Heroaen merchants, lives and sleeps in the back of his shop. "It happened a little before midnight," he recalled. "Thinking back on it, the noise was loud, urgent and strange. But it sounded so far off, I thought I was hearing it in a dream." Similarly, the remaining five residents recalled the intrusion of a sudden pounding of knuckles against wood. And like the drowsy apothecary, none had a clear notion of why they hadn't bothered to answer. Collectively, the dream was becoming the Heroaen nightmare.

But not every door the Commander ran to was unfamiliar. A week before the disturbance, Palome had stood in her parlor and watched her former lover pack his things. "He was leaving me to move across the street—to the old soap factory," Palome explained, without bitterness, though not without wonder. She added, "It was the last place he lived and slept." Of the night of the pounding on her door, she recalled only that, "It happened very late, and sounded like the knock of a drunk." Assuming its cause was a hopeful customer, Palome ignored it. "It was my off-duty night," she explained, belying a woman who gave freely of her body, but not her time.

Further down the alley, inside a balcony above the street, Antigone turned twice, adjusting herself in the bed. In the sleepy confusion, she had not understood that, in calling her name, his voice conveyed the unreality of a whisper only because of the deception created by distance. Carried up from the street below, it had dissipated by the time it reached her, invoking the lightness of dream. But in fact, the call had been too real.

Stricken with an optical illusion (the by-product of his urgency under the pressure of time), the Commander mistook the door of Antigone's building for the heavy wooden portal of the factory, where, after the long hours of making soap, they had stood in quiet anticipation of the wind. When it ushered in the sandstorm, he had pulled her beneath the cover of an awning where they hid their faces from the dust. And now, in the final sprint for shelter, it was toward Antigone that he ran. He was confounded, however, by the presence of the doorway, so resembling the entry to the factory he'd already passed. The memory, or mix-up of the doorways, marked precisely the moment when the Commander cried out her name—a scream rehearsed in countless, terrible dreams, without ever recognizing the sound. His voice exploded in a crackle of thunder which had no echo, but was followed by a flash of lightning that was no more that the burst of fire from the barrel of a gun, repeated by the flashes of several other guns.

With the assassins closing in, the Commander pressed his face against the door. His fist had been raised and clenched when the first bullet struck, shattering the bones of his back. The weight of his knuckles then fell like a single massive rock hurled against the portal. With chest pinned to the door by the force of what had hit him, the Commander spread his hands. He froze in that position until, at the expiration of that instant, simultaneous volleys struck him low, shattering both his kneecaps. Metal kept coming in waves, spattering pieces of him against the surface of the door which never did open. His agony was desperate—appearing indefinite. And yet, relative to the duration of things, it was staggeringly brief. According to science, the event spanned the mere fraction of a second.

Above him, inside the balcony of a third floor apartment of the building, Antigone stirred and quietly went back to sleep. Later, when asked to recall the incident, she would only say, "I heard a commotion in the street."

PART III

STREET

CHAPTER TEN

POISONS

CORPSE SMELL

CENTRAL SQUARE, Hero — It began as a twitch in the nostril, the prickle at the beginning of a sneeze. But with the coming of the heat wave, it had surged into the torment of a city, seeping in through tiny cracks of even the most conscientious of households, where every last door and window had been slammed and bolted. The efforts of citizens against the onslaught came to nothing, as, on the third day, the air continued to swell with the rotting compost of death. "At first, I assumed it had to be a rodent in an advanced stage of decay," a landlord told me. "But it was more than that; something not right with the stink. I had no way of explaining it to the tenants." Time stagnated in coordination with the odor, until even the arms of clocks had been anchored to their faces, immovable as ships withering against the dock.

Three nights after the killing, I sat in the middle of my room, chained to the chair as if by a pair of iron talons. Overhead, tribes of flies encircled my head, displacing air in swirls of silvery vapors. By this time, even the flies had grown plump from the stench. Through the ferocity of their buzzing, I sensed their preparation to zoom in like daws and start pecking at the skin of my eyelids. At any moment, the room and every living matter in it might spontaneously rupture from the severity of the heat. I slumped over, letting gravity transport me to the bed. I was just dosing off before the alarm clock burst with its menacing buzzer—a jolt even for someone partially awake. At 5 AM, barely having slept, I had even less appreciation for what time it was. I would have attempted to sit up, except for being unable to disentangle myself from the bed sheet, which had wrapped several times around me and was pasted to my skin. Instead, I lay there resigned to my present condition—a set of limbs held in restraint and a brain tied up in knots.

All the while, the sleep-in at The Square dragged on. I doused myself with water, already warm as it spurt out of the tap, then dressed and prepared myself to go there—descend to the pit—to wrestle the odor for another day.

DECREE

From the beginnings of the massive protest, public officials had decided to handle the public's anger by going along with it. Namely, this meant accepting the people's assumption that the body plundered from the pauper's grave indeed was that of the Commander. But that left the issue of how it originally got there. To divert attention from the question, The Authority decided to toss out its own smoke cloud, and it took the shape of a formal decree. With a sting in its eye, the body politic would have its chance to read the writing on the wall. Published on scrolls and posted throughout the city, the edict called the removal of the body "a criminal act," and alternately, "a prank." It declared, in big stick terms, that the perpetrators will be caught and punished.

Perhaps it's easy to view the governors' decree as a maneuver driven by fear—and supported by the desire to point out a scapegoat. It is the motivation of the crowd that is difficult to ascertain. Within twenty-four hours of the posting of the edict, they answered it by stoning their chosen victim in The Square. "The man was an informant, a traitor," a protester told me. "He got his due." It can be surmised, I guess, that the murder was a ritual act of vengeance. But it's one thing to show defiance in the midst of a rebellion. It's another thing, entirely, to hold a dead man hostage.

I was in The Square when the scuffle broke out between employees of the Sanitation Division and irate protesters stirring up the crowd. After three hours of nonproductive negotiation, the sanitation workers left—without retrieving the body they had ventured in for. Three days passed while the victim continued to rot, the mob erecting a scaffold to showcase the corpse as trophy.

Like a chain reaction, the Commander and Lieutenant had met their deaths within weeks of one another. "I don't understand it," the sanitation employee confided. "They had both been rebels, 'brothers in the struggle' was what they said." Reflecting on his own words, he shrugged. "We can see that is all very nice. But what happens when brother splits from brother? I'll tell you. It cuts a lesion in the skin that once had bound them—a sucking wound that can't be closed." He made a slash to his forearm with the blade of the other hand. "Betrayal breeds its own contagion," he said, his palms tracing the shape of an expanding balloon. "This quickly, it infects the whole city."

I have seen for myself what can happen when two brothers collide in battle, each one slaying the other. In a pattern established since ancient times, one is cast by fate (and crowd opinion) as the martyr, to be feted and paraded on shoulders through the streets of the town. Just as surely, the other will be condemned to rot in the sun, in full public view, making a sweet morsel for vultures. But an even funnier thing happens when the setting is moved to Hero. Details of the story are muddied by the heat and the intransigence of the dust bowl. It may be that the men were brothers not by blood, but by

some other kind of kinship. And maybe they did not exact each
other's death with their own hands, but it becomes clear, in
hindsight, how each did make the other's undoing.

I see now how the fate of the second corpse is traced back to
what happened to the first. The path beginning with the state's
assassination of the Commander, and its subsequent decision
to retain the body, would culminate in the stoning death of
the devoted Lieutenant who had, in the end, betrayed him.
Far from personal, the incident in The Square was merely the
vengeful reaction of the masses against a state that insulted and
oppressed them. Poorly had the authorities understood, even
then, how their thoughtless act of interference had stomped on
the will of the people, and aborted the drama of their heroic
tradition. By denying them the ritual of the martyr's burial,
the governors had inflicted a humiliation impossible to bear.
The crowd, for their part, would be satisfied with no less than
a killing for a killing; in the end, the ransom of a corpse for a
corpse.

DEGREES OF DESPERATION

There are different shades of desperation, and they come at
you from different angles. I turned over a fair number as I
approached The Square with mounting dread. In my fourth
day adrift inside the labyrinth, I continued to track the phantom
footsteps of the body politic. But they had not formed imprints
so much as stains. In them, I sought to read—and reconstruct—
not only the chain of events leading up to murder, but to
understand what drove them. From every angle, the killing was
a desperate act. And yet, as I was bound to discover, it had also
been premeditated, calculated and, above all—waited for.

But my first shock of the day happened as I came within view
of the obelisk. It was becoming illuminated by the sun just then
peaking over the mountain ridges of the borderland. In a word,
the effect was breathless. Even under siege—by outsiders, or

by its own citizens—the city retains an air of the untouchable, endowed with a beauty so strong it can afford to be forgiving.

Forgiveness, of course, was not foremost in the hearts and minds of the mob. Arriving at The Square, I resolved to confront the body politic—and not back down until I got inside its head. I vowed to accomplish this even at the cost of slaying the hissing, coiled strands of its hair…

But first, the coffee. I decided that my chances of success—indeed, survival—would be greatly increased with an early morning's hit of coffee. From the counter at Rix, I noted, impassively, the unimpeded view of The Square afforded by its wall-to-wall window. It would have been one of the last sights taken in by the Lieutenant. "He stopped here," the waitress confirmed, "like he did every afternoon." She had detected nothing unusual about his behavior. "He called for a plate of eggs—and it didn't matter what the hour of day—morning, afternoon, midnight—it was always eggs. He'd say, 'A good fried egg is worth a thousand words.' He was picky about how he liked them—crispy and dripping with oil. On that day, he had no complaints." Only then did she recall, "When finished, though, he just stood and put his money on the table. Getting to the exit, he looked confused and asked me for the bill—as if he hadn't paid. Looking back, it seems peculiar. But at the time, I didn't think too much of it."

Neither did one of the regular diners—the chess player—attach significance to the moment the Lieutenant paused to linger in front of the door. The customer thought, rather, that the departing Lieutenant appeared to be in a good mood, or at least, in no particular hurry. "The view of The Square is spectacular," the chess player pointed out. "Naturally, he took a moment to enjoy it. Even commented on how blue the sky was."

Or possibly noted, without suspicion, the amassing crowd.

BULL'S HEAD

From his unimpeded view of The Square, the Lieutenant did not see how at its center the "body politic" was quickly degenerating into the "mob"—or that its form had been misshapen by rage. He remained unsuspecting even as, strolling through the crowd with his usual swagger, the first stone struck him below the collar bone. From where and whom the first stone was cast will likely never be known.

An even greater mystery is how the Lieutenant could have been so innocent—or oblivious—to the danger that faced him. He would have been aware, as well as anyone, of the cause of the public's discontent. But that they clamored for a fallen hero he had taken a hand in befalling did not seem to phase him. I can only suggest that the Lieutenant, in his own mind, had not committed any wrongdoing—a denial that spares the self guilt and regret. Rather, as he had insisted during our interview that morning, he had delivered the Commander into the hands of his enemies for the sake of the war effort.

"He was a good man," the Lieutenant had commended. "Loyal and fearless. We relied on him for such a great deal. Then came the year of the 'peace summit'—a babble leading nowhere. Even so, the talks had their purpose. That was to convince our leaders to sell low—to settle for scraps—for no reason than because our people were tired of dying. Since that time, he was never the same. In the end, I could see him won over by the talking. We can't afford this. In hard times," he rebuffed, "we can't afford that kind of mercy. Once let into the garden, mercy grows like a weed." Shrewdly, the Lieutenant wagered that I would be of use to him as a media tool—through which he proposed to broadcast his story. Far from traitor, the Lieutenant saw himself as the redeemer of his cause, the rising champion of his beset nation. What I don't think he expected was to wind up, in twisted fashion, as its martyr. And I can't help but wonder how the crowd knew of the Lieutenant's betrayal before I'd gotten the chance to publish his shocking disclosure. Then again, he didn't appear to perceive the need to keep it a secret. Maybe he'd even bragged about it to fellow fighters—or to the neighbors. Apparently, the Lieutenant had believed himself immune to the ramifications of public opinion. In reality, the word on the street spreads like its own contagion. Just as the sanitation worker foretold, "This quickly, it infects the whole city."

The Lieutenant had gone to The Square to visit the pet store. There, he purchased a bag of seed with which to feed the birds. On days when he started to feel idle, the Lieutenant would climb to the roof of his building where, like a paranoid sentry, he'd place a steel bar across the jam of the door. Then, gazing out over the city's tarred chimneys, he felt like the king of Hero. And on such days when he started to feel idle, he wondered, as he often did, what had happened to the foam of his war. In the beginning, it was a rich lather like the hunger of a dog. But it seemed to have dissolved to a thin surface of disconnected bubbles, bursting at the touch. Lamentably, the war had reduced to the spent water of another bucket's dirty laundry.

WHEN THE SECOND STONE struck him in the eye, the Lieutenant lost his balance—and accidentally scattered the bag of seed he had purchased for the feeding of the birds. Staggering backward, he sought to increase the distance between himself and the enveloping masses. But it would prove a fatal decision, for it formed the clearing that made it possible for his assailants to cast the remainder of the stones—without getting hit themselves. The pelting battered and reshaped the victim who, by this time, no longer had the appearance of a man. A blinded beast with bloodied bull's head, he began to slip and lose his footing. Inside the darkened corridors of the labyrinth, an unidentifiable groan was followed by the punctured aching of a scream.

CHAPTER ELEVEN

PERSUASIONS

IMPARTIAL

PRISON, Hero — We had barely taken our seats, facing each other with the steel bars between us.

"I can see you're making an effort to be fair. But at some point," Hektor posed, "you must decide whether you're defending the rebels—or the traitors of rebels." Then his cool analysis turned to indictment when he asked, with disarming bluntness, "Whose side are you on?"

"I couldn't begin to tell you," I said, "because, frankly, I don't know."

"You must have some idea."

"I don't need to take sides," I maintained. "I dislike everyone."

"That's honest enough."

"Besides, I forfeited the right to choose sides when I accepted this job, better yet, this dubious profession. At least that's what they told me."

"Perhaps," he murmured. "But is it enough? To stay impartial, I mean."

"And all I can say is that, from what I've seen, hate is counter-productive. It only reinforces misery—yours and, no doubt, theirs."

"Well, so long as it increases *theirs*."

He meant his enemies—a loose confederation of colonial officials and their Heroaen sycophants. But on hearing his words, I began to despair that "they" would ever again let Hektor out of prison. Alternately, though, there was the all-pervasive "they" of the street. Of the latter category, I notified Hektor of his growing reputation. "They want to celebrate somebody," I explained. "As one of the rebels left standing, you're next in line."

"I'm sorry to hear it," Hektor bemoaned, showing his distaste for fame. "Truth is, I'm still trying to figure out how I got here."

"According to my information, you were captured just minutes after the Commander was killed," I said—getting no thanks for the reminder.

Okay, so times are funny. In The Square rots a dead guy who thought himself a hero—only to find out too late that the rest of the world did not agree. In the prison rots a man who doesn't consider himself a hero, while in the street, they persist in saying that he is. At best, the formula remains an enigma. The first clue, however, may be sought in the motivations of the doomed Lieutenant. Based on what he told me on the morning of that fateful day, he clearly believed the time had come for the war to make room for a new leadership. Presumably, with the Commander out of the way, the Lieutenant saw himself as the best man to step into those empty (and very large) shoes. It would prove a costly fantasy. Incredible as it seems in hindsight, the Lieutenant managed to overestimate the mob's capacity for forgiveness as much as he underestimated the reach of its vengeance. But if the result of his ambition was blindness, it was only part of the larger fog the war had done so well creating. And that's about as much clarity as we are likely to get.

Meanwhile, my article based on the conversation with the Lieutenant—in the only interview he would ever give—contributed very little to the public debate. Its only effect, in addition to annoying Hektor, was to expose an intrigue within the rebel ranks that ordinary people already knew about; moreover, had already passed sentence. Their indifference became clear when, at the scene of the ongoing protest, I observed the pages of my story employed to a more sensible use—as paper fans against the stagnation and the heat.

The sleep-in at The Square was now heading into its twenty-first day. Bizarrely, the mob had yet to set forth terms to resolve the standoff. And aside from the occasional calls for food and medicine, the body politic (through its representatives) announced no list of demands. What became clear, however, was that the stoning of the Lieutenant was neither spontaneous—nor accidental. "Twenty-four hours before it happened, I began hearing whispers of a rumor," a spectator at the scene recalled. "And once the idea caught on, it spread like a fever. I couldn't approve of it myself, and got a sick feeling. That's when I decided to go home. Later, hearing the news, I got a shudder. Just then, the heat wave began to blow in the smell."

Creeping into musty attics, neglected cupboards, and the food supply, it carried with it the suffocation of a city.

WITNESS

"I want Hero to breathe again," Antigone sighed. While the air continued to throb with the pulse of its own uncivil odor, she opened the confession I sensed she'd been trying to tell me all along. It explains why, on my next visit to the prison, I did not peer though steely bars at the battle-scarred face of a veteran, but at the childlike visage of a girl. She had given herself up to authorities on the belief that what was happening to the city was all her fault. It then took me twenty-four hours to negotiate access to her through the requisite "fees."

Looking a bit forlorn, but without any real hint of worry, Antigone expressed less interest in her own situation than in attempting to understand the acts of others. As we talked, she seemed bemused. "I do not believe people are bad for being caught in a bad situation," she said. "It is not the people who are bad. It is the situation. If I did not believe this, I could not forgive anyone."

It was not exactly clear to whom she meant to direct that forgiveness. We were, of course, in Hero—where a sentiment as precious as forgiveness is terminally in demand. Moreover, the candidates in line to receive it are many. Silently, I ran down the list of possible transgressors while Antigone glanced around me at no particular spot. With thoughts far away, she did not appear ready, as yet, to talk.

Not wanting to push her, I decided to skate over the moment by slipping her the parcel I managed to produce, like magic, from beneath the folds of my shirt. That sparked from her a smile of delight, however momentary. As had become my practice on visiting inmates, I arrived bearing a gift (not sausage or cigarettes this time—since Antigone indulges in neither; instead, I went with the more delicate offering of a book). Sophi had helped me select it from an expansive array of titles spanning the shelves of her sister's favorite book store. The possibilities were daunting, and I was stumped at the effort to narrow them down. "Romance, or adventure?" I asked blankly. "Better to go with adventure," Sophi advised. "The more outrageous, the better." We finally settled on a volume of classical tales featuring one-eyed monsters and the like. "That's a good one," Sophi confirmed. "She likes monsters best."

It was no accident, then, that Antigone had plenty of monsters to contend with. At the top of the list would be the CID agents masquerading as lawyers. "They ask me over and over where I was on this day, that hour. Sometimes I tell them, and sometimes I don't remember. I say that I am tired, but they just keep asking." I was familiar with CID's tactics of interrogation, where repetition is used to distort and confuse, and ultimately, to break down the will. What the agents could not account for was Antigone's exceptional strength of will. More than anything, that's what concerned me. As I studied her, I recognized signs of fatigue. In addition to the cloudiness of her brow, there was the distant, sad look I have seen too often in the eyes of prisoners.

Leaving her with the gift of a book, I resigned myself to pulling little from Antigone that day. She was no more inclined to reveal to me than to the agents the information that every one of us was seeking. Each, for our own reasons and motives, sought to discover—before anyone else did—the resting place of the Commander. Collectively, we had embarked on a corpse chase of the grandest scale. But it was not the absurdity of the race that disturbed me. It was the dismal feeling that I was being drawn into a contest for Antigone's secrets—if not her soul.

Antigone's only crime, if you can call it that, was to see something she perhaps should not have. It was an odyssey beginning at the tree where she once disclosed to me her unusual intimacy with the Commander. Fittingly, it was also the place where, concealing herself in one of the branches, she had held her round-the-clock surveillance of the building across the street. The morgue—over-run with protesters by day—was abandoned in the evenings to its own nocturnal gloom. Among all of Hero's citizens, Antigone alone witnessed the removal of the Commander's body by two men attired in well-cut suits. Fearing connection with the same pair who came to see her in the prison, she added, "They were dressed like lawyers." Equally astute was her reasoning that there are only so many destinations for a corpse in Hero. Taking the back roads, she simply out-stealthed the "lawyers" by arriving at the location before they did. In the pauper's graveyard, she hid herself behind a mound where, beneath the silvery moonlight, she beheld the clandestine burial that was at once more than a theft—and worse than a crime. In Antigone's eyes, the act she witnessed was a sacrilege.

Early on, I put forth Heroaens as a people judged less by the lives they live than by how they are treating the dead. By a related principle, the outlaw of today can become the hero of tomorrow. One has only to spend enough time in Hero to make the connection, but getting there is a special challenge if you are an outsider trying to follow the contortions of the local logic. In making the attempt, I saw it all begin with the state's detainment of the corpse of the Commander, coupled with the prohibition of his funeral. It's mystifying, I suppose, that no one disputed the fact that the state killed him (it was taken for granted). The outstanding issue (the only one people seemed to care about) was The Authority's ill-formed decision to appropriate the corpse; worse yet, to dump it into an unmarked pauper's grave. I then contributed the equally ill-formed decision to write about it. In effect, I had triggered an escalation of the riots. The state responded, as states do, with the fullness of its military might—sending its army to seize control of hot spots, conduct mass arrests of rebels, and harass their sympathizers (where I managed to be included in the net). That explains, I'm sure, why I'd been set upon by thugs. With dismay, I watched the mob's occupation of the city plaza turn into an ugly reprisal against the oppressions of the state. At critical mass now, Hero is on the brink of an all-out civil war. In the textbook sense, it is "collaborators" versus "patriots"—or something like that.

None of this matters to Antigone. Assigned by fate as well as tradition, she has simply embraced her role as the unrepentant outlaw of today; and, with the way things go, the bona fide hero of tomorrow. I can only assume that she was compelled by conscience to confess, even if her sole "crime" was removing and reburying the body. Surely, she could not have foreseen how doing so would ignite the imagination of the world.

MEDIA WAR

The labyrinth had trapped me for real this time, because no matter which direction I turned, I'd come face-to-face with my own part in the tragedy. I don't mean that, as a tool of the media,

I'd allowed myself to be manipulated in the interest of chasing the story. What bothered me was having lent a direct hand in some of that manipulation. Pea Nuts insists that conflicts of conscience are "a reporter's fate, the bargain we all signed up for." And truth, so far as we stumble upon it, rarely fails to carry its own load of consequences. "It's like buying a pile of diamonds," he proposed, "not knowing if half the pile is glass. No one makes us a guarantee, Teheda."

In equally self-rebuking terms, Luis and I got together at Zax to try to gain perspective. Many drinks into the session, we sunk to taking simple jabs at one another's lapses, if not in ethics, than in judgement. Like obedient soldiers, we'd both held the front lines of The Chronicle and Cosmos in the media war-within-the-war. In the race for headlines, this entailed the use of sometimes ruthless tactics. And yet, in spite of his boasts to the contrary, Luis is not an altogether heartless man. "It's too bad it had to all come down on the girl," he said, sharing concern for Antigone and what might await her. She was our sacrificial innocent. Carried on the wave of the media cyclone, Antigone alone made no conscience effort to direct it. And yet, she is the most influential figure to emerge from the mess, by virtue of her single-minded determination to fulfill a private— if somewhat mystifying—conviction.

"What do you think of Hero's track record for clemency?" I posed to Luis.

"Well, she violated an edict—the first of its kind in modern times, so no precedent has been established. In legal terms," he analyzed, "that's bad."

The fact that the law was passed retroactive to the crime did little to dissuade its proponents from vicious prosecution. Since arresting Antigone, the authorities had been vacillating between threats and bribes, even dangling the possibility of a plea bargain. All the while—as Antigone herself informed me—she had yet to see the inside of the courtroom. Instead, her case seemed, in an alarming way, to be playing out in the newspapers. In free market fashion, state spokesmen parceled out breaking announcements to the highest bidder through their extra-legal "contacts." A competing buyer in the auction, Luis once again beat me to the headline.

He had learned that, to resolve the situation which burgeoned from a political problem into a public health crisis, the authorities were "willing to bargain." In the interest of restoring civil order, its spokesman told him, the state was prepared to pay the reparation the body politic had been demanding—if not articulating—all along. "It has been determined that the people must regain the deceased member whose unknown whereabouts have created such a stir." Within the state's scenario, the only obstacle to "peace" had become Antigone—believed to possess sole knowledge of the present location of the corpse.

I had the regrettable role of reporting this development to the notorious prisoner. She'd been placed under quarantine. "They said it was to protect me from the smell," she reported, no doubt puzzled. In reality, it was a transparent euphemism for solitary confinement—a punitive measure designed to cut her off from the outside world.

"They've given you an ultimatum," I informed her. "Give up the Commander—or face the penalty of death."

TO LIVE

I left Antigone at the prison only to return later with a reinforcement. Sophi was stoic in the taxi. I'd brought her with me reluctantly, but in the desperate bid that her presence was more likely to influence her sister than mine would. "Antigone is not about to change her mind," Sophi stated with desolate frankness, "not even for me." She agreed to go along for no reason other than to give me peace of mind. So from the sidewalk, we advanced toward a stream of rush hour traffic. Responding to my flailing arms, the driver of a stylishly-dented vehicle screeched to a halt. Hastily, we packed ourselves into the passenger cabin only to face the back of his head through the narrow slits of vertical iron bars. In uncanny fashion, they seemed to forecast our destination. Arriving at the prison, I took Sophi's hand and sped us up the promenade to a pair of looming, fortified gates.

Our urgency came out of a determination, perhaps naïvely, that we might persuade a girl to reverse a pre-fated decision. We had the solemn mission of convincing her to live. But at the visitor station, Sophi sat beside me saying little while I enumerated, out of a sense of helplessness, all the things Antigone must already have known she had to live for. I began by extolling obvious virtues—the love of a family and her upcoming marriage, for starters. "And then, there are the consolations of the moment," I said.

They are too painfully real. And even if Antigone didn't require reminding, I pointed out a few—from the volumes of her favorite books to the violet light of the Heroaen sunset. However, at the mention of these, she appeared to slip only deeper into melancholy. To my profound disappointment— and failure—Antigone would not be moved. For the first time in our brief, though enlightening, acquaintance, Antigone seemed impervious to simple pleasures. "This is not the time to be dwelling on such things," she stated. She believed, in earnest, that The Authority's proclamation was a "trick"—that regaining possession of the Commander's body, they would again defile it.

"So you'd die for the sake of protecting a corpse?" I posed. "Antigone, a corpse is just a dead thing. But you are alive."

"I don't want to die," Antigone defended, "but without dignity, we're not really living."

In the gravity of her voice and the somberness of her small, sallow face, I finally grasped the latent force—and full ferocity—of the Heroaen will.

And I'm not sure that I will ever recover.

DEBTS

I didn't have the heart to tell Luis that when it came to contacts, I was holding the ace card. I decided to play it by paying a call on the Mayor. We met in the courtyard of his posh office building, where, like a feudal lord, he snapped his fingers for an underling to fetch us a tray. It arrived displaying two demitasse cups and saucers accompanied by an assortment of miniature pastries. While I declined to indulge in the delicacies, he insisted that I at least sample the results of his new state-of-the-art cappuccino machine. Growing sentimental, he perused, with great satisfaction, his upscale surroundings. "Nostalgia and progress are dual blades of the sword," he said. "We invent things to shield us from nature; then seek solace by simulating what we have lost from the beginning. Take this courtyard, for example. See that dirt patch overgrowing with weeds?"

"Some people call them wildflowers."

"Well, they're history. Look there in a month and you'll see an electro-powered waterfall."

The Mayor's boast served as an echo-in-reverse of words once spoken by his eliminated rival. The former Commander explained to me, "A man can grow rich by his wits, so long as his lies remain invisible. For me, it is better to earn what I need with my hands. They are not hidden. You see this food I grasp? It is only a scrap, yet it sustains me. That man with his wealth? Even candy touching his mouth will choke him and turn to poison." He then observed, "Even so, he grows fat on the poison."

AFTER ACCEPTING my praises of the cappuccino, the Mayor got down to business. "I suppose you're here about the fate of the girl," he presumed—less out of clairvoyance than from having fielded a host of other eager journalists' calls. "I don't mind saying that some of my colleagues are fools—no better at reading the mood of the world community than of the mob in the street. What's going on in Hero hurts progress.

Naturally, our international sponsors are worried. They have threatened to hold back their aid. We are talking billions of dollars."

I sensed the Mayor's concern for the future of the electric fountain. My interest, of course, lay elsewhere. I asked, "What does it mean for the girl?"

The Mayor straightened his paisley silk necktie. "Under the circumstances, you can imagine my hesitance to speak to the press. Today, the information I give you means one thing—and one thing only." He made clear, and with predictable smugness, "In the future, you will owe me."

And I am a man tortured by my debts.

More importantly, I felt that I owed something to Antigone, though I continued at a loss of what to call it. Maybe, simply put, the word was "responsibility." As I once told Sophi, sometimes you have to take in order to give back. The problem was, since returning to Hero, I'd been doing a lot more taking than giving. Without scruples, I had appropriated Antigone's secrets in order to spill them to the world. Had it not been for the media whirlwind I gave a hand in stirring, Antigone would have spent her day very differently—browsing her favorite bookstore, exploring the mounds of the mystic desert, or climbing a tree.

Instead, she was meeting me at the visitor station, peering out through the rails of the security window. At least her escort had been kind enough to forego the handcuffs—for which I expressed gratitude by slipping him a couple of dollars. "Some of the guards are nice to me," Antigone reported. "They've been teaching me how to play cards. And this one, he even let me win a game." I guess that was to reassure me that not all of her jailors were bad.

"Your death sentence has been lifted," I informed her. "I heard it straight from the Mayor." She replied with a sigh. It was not the breath of relief as I'd expected, but of someone weighted with a burden.

"Antigone, the news is good," I pressed. "So what's the matter?"

"You still want me to tell them where the corpse is," she hedged. "That's the other reason why you're here."

"Perhaps," I admitted. "At least, I'm asking you to think about it. Antigone, the wounds of your city are deep. You alone have the power to heal them. You said there is a kind of death-in-living. But you also said you wanted Hero to breathe again. This city was beloved by the Commander. Giving him back to it may be the only way."

CHAPTER TWELVE

ALCHEMY

HERO'S PASS

MIDDLE DESERT, Hero — The next day just before
sundown, I began winding my way to Hero's Pass—the section
of the cemetery where Antigone had arranged for my meeting
with her outside "contact." Crossing the city, I retraced the
journey Sophi had showed me as part of our tour. Passing the
defunct railroad tracks, dilapidated warehouses, and burnt
coffee groves, each location called up her memories of a
childhood compromised by violent loss. But they recalled, too,
an idyllic land, erased from history even as it grew stronger in
the mind. Arriving at dusk, I waited under a clear sky, crackling
stars, and a bulbously luminous moon.

"Discovering perfection, Teheda? Or just beauty where you
never thought you'd find it?"

Her voice cut with the force of shattering crystal—divine,
immaculate, and as inexplicable as the sand it is made of.

"There is a certain power here," I agreed. "Something
atmospheric."

"Either that, or it's the heat," Sophi replied, her voice chiming a desert tune in my ear.

Her remark about the heat reminded me, if unnecessarily, that I was still in Hero—where identities are hidden, realities contradicted, and truths revealed without needing to be spoken.

It should have occurred to me that the most natural accomplices to a crime would be a pair of sisters. I must have been thrown off the scent by the implausibility of the details. The Commander had not been a small man; but rather, even by an athlete's standards, a colossus. How then were Antigone and Sophi, both so slight in stature, able to unearth and transport his body to Hero's Pass?

"We borrowed the old farmer's vegetable cart," Sophi confided. "He even hitched us up with the donkey."

I remained puzzled about the material evidence which had served as my first real clue.

"The toy shovel," I said, "discarded so carelessly beside the plundered grave. Why?"

"We had arrived just after sunset," she explained, "and started digging. Minutes later, we discovered how impractical it was to have relied on that ridiculous tool. In disgust, we tossed it, then started to go at the dirt with our hands."

And so, they labored side-by-side beneath the moonlight—a pair of hungry hyenas whose faces became spattered with dirt.

"We vowed to keep our act a secret, not only because of how strange it was, but because we were sisters. When Antigone decided to break the silence, there was nothing I could do to stop her. So I pleaded for us to go to the police together, at least let me do the talking. But Antigone said, 'stay out of it.' From the beginning, the whole thing had been her idea."

That disclosure made sense. But another matter didn't.

"The day you showed me Hero's Pass," I recalled, "you must not have expected that we'd wind up at the pauper's section. Seeing the empty grave site made you nervous—especially when I noticed the shovel. That's why you picked it up and put it in your pocket. Didn't you think that would make me suspicious? If I was smarter, that is."

"I had to take it back," Sophi explained. "It had Antigone's name carved into the handle."

If her admission made them less-than-perfect criminals, that's not what bothered me.

"When I first came to your door and told you I was a reporter, you had a secret to protect. Yet you agreed to talk to me. Why? Sophi, was it only a game?"

"Not a game," she said. "Only, perhaps, the unexpected urge to help you."

At once, I understood why I had fallen in love with her. Not only was she Sophi, goddess of cool intelligence, humor, and wit; a marvel of understatement. But she was Sophi, the girl whose smile trails off slightly toward one side. And finally, she was Sophi, the silk thread wrapped around a core of steel. "I don't know why," she continued, "except maybe, because you had come here to learn the truth—about the Commander, about us, about living and dying in Hero. And I guess because, in a funny sort of way, I trusted you."

I had no more questions.

HEADLINES

Flowers do not belong in Hero. At least, that's what the law says. In retaliation against the Great Uprising, the colonial government slapped trade restrictions on certain kinds of produce. Included on the list were ordinary fruits and vegetables, the more common breeds of potatoes, exotic medicinal roots, and oddly enough, flowers. Even the homegrown variety were summarily declared illegal. To this day, the no-flower policy is more effectively enforced than the prohibition of narcotics. Long puzzled by the status of flowers as a dangerous substance, I assumed they were more potent as symbol than substance. When I asked Antigone what she thought flowers represented for Heroaens, she said "hope," then regarded me with pity as if

I were a simpleton. I suppose the answer could not have been more obvious. To this day, the restrictions on produce have not been lifted. Ostensibly, they were designed to flush out rebel elements of the population, who were supposed to grow tired of deprivation and simply give up. That didn't happen. In fact, a wave of new factions sprung up. Hungry ones.

The embargo has been in effect for most of Antigone's lifetime. And yet, she never stopped believing in flowers, even if it was true, as Sophi said, that the flowers were nothing but plastic. But on the day of their brother Tibolt's funeral, the flowers were as real as they needed to be. Clasped lovingly in a young girl's hands, they could not have made a more fitting gesture of goodbye. In a war where youth is the easiest casualty, the toy bouquet never did go back to the arms of Antigone's little doll bride. But, recycled from hero to hero, the flowers make a uniquely pertinent symbol—poignant on the one hand, pragmatic on the other. They're not exactly fancy, but they get the job done. And plastic, they may well be. But like Antigone, I dare anyone to deny that they are real.

While it has faded in color, the bouquet again adorns the kind of humble but dignified headstone that commemorates the passing of a martyr. Almost absurdly, its stiff petals fend against the wind. At the site, I found the flowers oddly peaceful, and their presence nothing short of a miracle. The stone itself bears the simple inscription, "HERO"—scrawled in large, block-style letters with a crayon. To the fog of existing contradictions, I contribute my own. If the Commander was a man who believed in violence, he was also a man who believed that mostly, it hurt the wrong people. Either way, except for the briefest reprieve, he had found no exit from its labyrinth.

By the multitudes, Antigone herself has been labelled a martyr and hero. By the state, she has been cast as the pathetic victim, manipulated by extremists and exploited by the media. And by the international press, she has been hailed as a champion of nonviolent resistance. But for me, she is no less than the waif who operated outside the system, and by a mixture of innocence, will, and indifference, appears to have won. As for the victory, she's indifferent to that, too. All Antigone cares about is that she has fulfilled a private sense of duty, owed to a man she barely had the chance to know, but who had unlocked for her the mystical properties of soap.

For my part, I dutifully made the Commander's grave site public with another Chronicle headline. Satisfied that their fallen patriot had gotten the respect that was due him, the body politic then answered its cue by releasing the traitor's corpse they'd held in ransom for a remarkable twenty-six days. In the final bargain with authorities, the protesters also secured Antigone's release from detention, then celebrated with a massive parade. In the wake of the carnival-like festivities— replete with clowns—the jubilant crowds simply dispersed to their homes. City workers rushed into the plaza to clean up the garbage left by the sleep-in. "We had to use the strongest chemical solvents," the sanitation director explained, "to wipe away lingering traces of the dead man."

The day after, I found The Square not only sterile, but deserted. Elsewhere, the streets resumed a normal—if somewhat eerie—sense of calm. More bizarre was Hollow Bones' observation that, in spite of the recent fanfare, only a handful of mourners actually made it over to Hero's Pass to visit the Commander's grave site. I guess the role of the hero in Hero is less about the man than about the need to feed a people's insatiable imagination. I long ago formulated that Heroaens are judged foremost by their treatment of the dead. I now can see that a man is also judged less by the acts of his life than by the service of his death. It may be a distinctly Heroaen equation, or just the hero by a universal definition.

WIND

Heroaens have a special relationship with nature. In a pronounced habit here, people are quick to point out that, in spite of mankind and its foibles, it is the wind that rules the day. With as much cruelty as it rakes up the sands to dump on our heads and clog our membranes, it can soothe our heat-worn bodies with the sudden flush of a summer breeze. Some days its force is gentle, sometimes mocking, but nearly always it is intoxicating with the fragrance of something far away. I was learning, like the locals, to give wind the special deference it deserves; and maybe, to surrender to the deeper mystery of its motives. I could no more understand the reasons for its wrath than for its bounty; just knew that both were wayward and unpredictable. The only thing I could do, then, was brace myself for the inevitable outcome—that the same wind that gave me Sophi was now about to take her away.

A brisk wind began blowing early in the morning. At the hour of lunch, it could be seen whipping up loose particles into hail-like balls of lint tripping along the sidewalk. And by late afternoon, it settled to a delicate bluster so serene it was disconcerting. All was to remind me of its vigor, I guess. Or its ubiquity. I know I have never felt more at its mercy. For the moment, though, I was busy watching it tousle the wisps of hair Sophi did not bother to brush from her eyes. And I can remember how, gingerly stepping over cobblestones of the broken pavement, Sophi was looking at the ground.

"It is a very real danger, isn't it?" she started out.

With innocence, I asked, "Which part?"

"Running out of all the hurt that makes you write."

Suddenly, we were no longer talking about Hero—or about the war, for that matter. With horror, I realized I had been effectively backed into a corner. So long subjected to the prying gaze of journalists' cameras, a Heroaen was now turning her lens *on me*.

"I can't apologize for that, Sophi. Writing is what I do."

The statement was more blunt than I intended. And who knows what I intended when adding, "I think there's more to it than that."

"Yes, I know," she said. "There will always be *more of the pain*."

When it comes to playing with words, I had more than met my match. Elegant, impeccable Sophi, so full of anger and venom—and so unafraid of telling the truth. "There will be more pain, always," she repeated. "So don't worry. When you run out of your own supply, you can always get more from others—especially if you stay in Hero. But you won't stay, will you?"

If she felt used, I didn't exactly blame her. Sophi, in the gentlest possible way, had become the war. She was its hurt; its sad seduction, too. More than that, she had become Hero. Sophi. Her war. Her city. All are jealous mistresses, I've learned. They sucked me into the void, then filled me up again; with what, I still don't know. And I'd gone along with the seduction, for no better reason than to feel desperate, willing, and confused—the few ways of still knowing I'm alive. I am certain that I will think of Sophi often, just as I will think of her city.

Weeks went by. Then came the point where I decided that the most exciting thing I could be in life was a recluse. I spent lightless days and sleepless nights shuffling through the mountains of notes I had collected. Feverishly, I sought to condense the war into a single, coherent volume—and just couldn't find the words. I next saw Sophi in the street, walking toward me in her graceful, deliberate fashion. We stood facing one another a short distance from the street lamp, on the corner of the busiest intersection in The Square. A man of words, I again could not find the right ones. Finally, it was Sophi who broke the impasse.

"You look like a little boy, hiding hands inside your pockets. Could it be that you have lost something?"

"Perhaps," I shrugged.

"Poor Teheda," she said mildly.

"And poor Sophi," I replied.

"You are right. Forever, I'll be searching this life for love, and you for pain. Both of us doomed to be unhappy."

She flashed the same conspiratorial smile with which she'd once promised to show me the true face of Hero, the one buried in the depths of the city. The difference was, her smile was a little sadder this time.

HERO'S LEGACY

My afternoon improved little when Pea Nuts called me into his office for a chat about the special report I'd just turned in. "Do you know what the problem is with your stories?" he posed. "They are missing a bad guy. I'm confused as to whom I'm supposed to blame for things. Everyone is a well-meaning victim of chance, and no one really means to do anybody else in. Where are the festering resentments?"

Normally, I might have said "Twenty yards down the hallway," and Pea Nuts would have laughed over the thinly veiled reference to Zoey's desk. We both understood, of course, that the nature of her animosity toward me had been good-natured enough. In recent days, moreover, her attitude was softening considerably. I even found her whistling a tune while moving her belongings into the larger desk that she had so long fixed her eye on. Much to her credit, Zoey's investigation of the soap factory had finally propelled her byline onto The Chronicle's front page. In it, she'd exposed a deal struck between commercial developers and bureaucrats to convert the old soap factory into Hero's first mega-store. Not wanting to risk the public's further discontent, the bureaucrats backed down and revoked the deal—even terminating a number of its ranking members who'd been singled out as scapegoats. At the end of the day, Hero's soap factory was saved. Moreover, in addition to Zoey finally getting her promotion—and my desk—I'm considering nominating her for Reporter of the Year.

My own flight as bureau chief in Hero was concluding like a wayward comet—with more sputter than crash. I simply packed my scant possessions into a suitcase before setting out to hire the taxi...that would transport me to the bus...that would take me to the ferry...that would eventually deposit me at the airport. I had accepted the offer of a new assignment: covering a multi-national dispute over fishing rights in arctic waters. At least I could look forward to the climate change.

Walking out the glass doors of The Chronicle, however, I succumbed to the nagging impulse that, before taking my departure of Hero, there was yet another person I needed to see. Inside the atrium of the soap factory, I discovered Antigone sitting on the tiny elm wood bench she had grown so fond of. "Have you come to say goodbye?" she asked, if only noting my presence out of the corner of her eye. When I said, "Yes," her gaze remained fixed on a ribbon of silver light beaming in through the arching, narrow window. Finally, in a voice barely above a whisper, she exclaimed, "Don't you love this place?"

I did not think for a moment that she meant Hero. What did Antigone care about Hero, a battered city that time has practically forgotten? This was Antigone, and she could only have been talking about the factory that had become her peculiar passion. With my own eyes, I scanned the dusty walls, the soap-encrusted barrels.

"It has its charm," I assured her.

"I think magic," she insisted. "It has magic. Or maybe, it just has life."

I wondered, suddenly, that if Sophi's search was for love, and mine for pain, what was it that Antigone looked for?

"Do you believe that life is magic?" I asked her.

"Are you teasing?"

"No, just asking."

Considering carefully, she replied, "Life isn't magic." Then, without any visible intention of reading my thoughts, she said, "It's a search for magic. Maybe the magic is in the searching." The entire time I stood there, Antigone hadn't once taken her eyes from the light. I left her to it—carrying away with me the image of a girl who seemed as much to be waiting as searching.

BY AFTERNOON, I was beginning to see that my desire to slip unnoticed out of Hero had been unrealistic. Having left Sophi at The Square and Antigone at the factory, I next directed the cabdriver to take me to the prison. It seemed only right that my journey conclude by way of a parting conversation with Hektor. In recording this chronicle, I have often thought back to our first interview, and how it had opened the way for the writing of this story.

"You asked if I consider myself a hero," he recalled. "I'm not sure I ever attempted to be one. All I know is how to do my work."

"Fair enough," I conceded.

"And now, it's my turn for asking you. My question is, do you consider yourself a happy man?"

"Relatively speaking, I can't complain," I answered. "Not much is missing from life that I don't expect to be."

"That's grim," he said.

"I know," I replied.

And we laughed, assuring ourselves of the dark and mutual understanding of two men standing in the half light. But the agreement was momentary. Yet dissatisfied, Hektor prodded further.

"Alright then, never mind about the happy. What I really want to know is, how goes living? For a free man, that is."

"A free man?" I rejoined. "What a concept. You are a prisoner of these bars, these walls. But the bars and walls are on the outside. You are a prisoner on the outside. Myself, I am imprisoned on the inside—by my own compulsions. I torment myself with questions for which there are no answers. Take morality, for example."

"Whether smart people deserve to live more than stupid people...stuff like that?"

"I don't give a damn about what anyone deserves," I said. "I'm more interested in the bigger question of why any of us are on the planet in the first place."

"If one thing is certain, it's that *I* don't know, either," Hektor replied. "And if I figure it out, I'm not going to tell anybody. Unless, of course, I patent the answer."

I don't doubt that someday, he'll do so. In the end, if anyone is capable of solving the age old riddle of man's existence, it will be Hektor. But first, he hoped to tackle a more immediate mystery. "It's amazing, isn't it, all the secrets a woman can hide?"

Forbidden to see his betrothed during her detention, he had to rely on the prison grapevine for all his news. As for the averting of Antigone's near catastrophe, he was visibly relieved, taking it as more proof that "the ladies are braver than we are. Maybe we should just hand the war over to them." I took that as a very real proposition, for which the only reply I could come up with was, "Yeah, but they would end it."

Of course, while I had been writing, life went on for him. In the interim, high level talks had been conducted between the Imperial Cabinet and representatives of the various Heroaen factions. Negotiating the release of prisoners had been included in the agenda. While the prospect of freedom had brought unprecedented hope to some of his cell mates, Hektor had largely ignored it. "Peace talks are like the seasons," he dismissed. "In a few weeks, the whole thing passes. And, as you can see, we are still here."

"Under the circumstances, then, how has it been?"

"Not too bad," he replied, his tone bordering on cheerful. "The rations are improving." I did not require specifics to understand that he was referring to the quality of the coffee.

"How about you, Teheda? Still tormented by your compulsions?"

"It's a matter of fate, I suppose."

"What will you do now that you have written your story?" he persisted.

"Move onto the next, what else? What will Hektor do?"

"That's easy," he stated flatly. "I'll try to live."

WHAT HERO MEANS TO ME

Hero means different things to different people.

While Antigone calls it a state of floating, Pea Nuts believes that Hero is a channel of the mind. For Sophi, it is a surreal, abandoned landscape; for myself, a definitively strange and convoluted journey. Hektor claims it is nothing more than a cardboard box with four walls and a poorly fitting lid. The

Commander's father suggests that Hero is only Purgatory in a constant state of flux. I suspect his son might have said that, in the end, our definitions are not important. What is important is what any of us wants from Hero, or from life—for what it's worth.

So, what does anyone actually *want* from Hero? Setting out one day to conduct the survey, I obtained a list of interesting answers. As for Hero being a channel of the mind, Pea Nuts contemplates jumping over to a different channel. Sophi hopes to populate her streets with smiling, happy people; the Commander's father welcomes the chance to quit his day job; and Hektor wants to expand the length and width of the box. Antigone reaches for something she cannot put a name to, but thinks she is content, for now, just to feel the longing.

I'm not sure what the Commander might have wanted. I would very much have liked to know. "There is no meanness here. Only pain," he'd told me, in a statement that summarized with simple eloquence that which, with thousands of words at my disposal, I could not. His remarks have come to strike me as prophetic, revealing an uncanny understanding of my eventual role in this strange drama. Out of courtesy, I had disclosed to him my imminent plans for leaving the country—making his the last interview of my brief stay.

"Had enough of us?" he gathered. "And who can blame you?" Then, more thoughtfully, "So, what happens now? You'll go back to your world, working hard in order to forget us. Time passes. Yet, as much as you try not to, you'll look back, again and again, to this city of Hero. You will think and write about us, the whole time, looking for the meaning. But I tell you this much. Hero will never make sense. And it will always get away from you."

BUS STOP

Surrounding this city are littered outposts. Both old and recent, their skeletons are in varying stages of decay. They are abandoned places, overlooking boulders and tremendous expanses of sand. I notice we are passing one after the other until arriving at the furthest extreme. There, a solitary soldier waves us through the check point, then slips imperceptibly back into the shade of his booth. Some distance later, the taxi finally lets me out at the brink of the ancient stone quarry— that famed dumping ground for the refuse of dreams. I pay the driver one last time, then watch the tires of his vehicle turn up dust as it is rolling away. From the rear view mirror, my driver gives me the playful gesture of a farewell salute. A busy man, he is no doubt off to pick up the next passenger on this endless journey of passengers.

But I, for now, have arrived at my destination. Like all destinations, it is transitional and temporary at best. I am at the bus depot—and am able to know it only because of the sign. That would be the weather-beaten plaque affixed to the stone. The stone itself is freakish in scale and, moreover, has been mysteriously positioned by the side of the road. However remote and indifferent, the spot serves as the only way to enter or leave Hero—*legally*, anyway.

Gazing down from the quarry's edge, I feel as if I am in the middle of a desert—an invisible one. It conceals itself beneath the skin of the city, and is formed by the layers of desolation that have accumulated over time. There are slivers of sunlight amidst the shadows and, mesmerized, I begin staring at the land. If I look long enough, squinting, I begin to see traces of the poetry long ago etched into the stones. At such moments, the world offers an illusion of coming together. I glimpse that there may even be a logic to things. I take this on faith because I am desperate to believe it.

And then, there is the evidence. Factually, it began with little more than a standard series of riots, accented by a face staring out from the black bars of a prison. Factor in another man's torn, discolored body—and the possibilities abound. In the end, all would point, improbably, to a toy shovel once belonging to a girl. I cannot claim that the evidence is other than murky. On the surface, it inspires little trust. Underneath, however, it conceals the reality of sieges; the inviolability of convictions; and the urgency of premeditated acts of honor. I still do not know whether, in fact or fiction, I have written the true story of this war. But I lack no confidence in what I've seen. Mostly, it's that Hero is about more than the futility of human conflicts and causes—because that much can be assumed. I now know that it's just as much about the courage of the obsession—to fight, to love, to bury.

As yet, I have been unable to reveal the dead by their actual names. And I am still unsure whether Hero is the crime mystery disguised as epic tragedy, or the epic tragedy masquerading as crime mystery. This is not an identity disorder so much as a suppleness of the view. What's more, maybe it really is hell and paradise all neatly wrapped into one.

Most importantly, though, I have given up coffee. It was quite the struggle, taking my body a whole week to figure out what was going on. Then, as if by magic, I slept for seventy-two hours straight before happily waking without the alarm clock. Maybe the apothecary was right. Every poison does contain its own antidote. After all, Hero does boil down to a weird concoction. Here and there, it tests the fragile balance of opposing forces that some say is the Eros and Thanatos; an obscure hint at the Yin and the Yang; or maybe, like Hektor's fighters, a rare agreement between contention and forgiveness.

In any case, it is hard to believe that I am finally leaving Hero. I turn away now from the momentary clarity—and coolness—of the quarry. Almost immediately, I am met by a wall. It is the heat pressing into the pores of my skin. Once more, my body reduces to a cutaway shape taken from the thickness of the air.

—J.R. Teheda